T0150601

NOTES FROM A WRITER'S BOOK

OF CURES AND SPELLS

Also by Marcia Douglas
Electricity Comes to Cocoa Bottom
Madam Fate

Heart-bottom thanks to L.F. and A.F.

NOTES FROM A WRITER'S BOOK

OF CURES AND SPELLS

A NOVEL BY

MARCIA DOUGLAS

PEEPAL TREE

First published in Great Britain in 2005, reprinted 2014

Peepal Tree Press
17 King's Avenue
Leeds LS6 1QS
England

© Marcia Douglas 2005, 2014

ISBN 9781845230166

All rights reserved
No part of this publication may be
reproduced or transmitted in any form
without permission

Supported using public funding by
ARTS COUNCIL
ENGLAND

"Because that's how the lizard like to walk."
– Muriel

CONTENTS

ROOT WORD

It's late and I'm up sweeping the kitchen. All day Alva's story has been on my mind. The strange odor of her tears fills the house, but for all my writing, I have not found her.

Just as I am about to lean the broom against the back door, ole Story-ma comes to me naked. Her sagged breasts swing back and forth like two pouches of magic; a long white beard hangs from her crotch down to her knees. Quick, I take the pen from behind my ear and write on my palm, *Tell mi Alva's secret.*

Ma takes my hand in hers and reads it, tracing the words with a tamarind finger.

"Walk your story round and around, full circle like a ripe starapple. One straight line might get you there, but you'll miss the crossings, and lose the story."

Story-ma disappears and I put my pen back behind my ear. Out in the yard, the sky is indigo as I shake the kitchen mat. I grip the corners like the reins of a chariot, my arms rising up and down. A slice of onion translucent as moon's skin falls to my feet and the little holes in the sky glisten like the wet sieve hanging over the sink; ground nutmeg and yellow cornmeal fill the air. Inside the asleep house, I spread the mat, a clean Orion, in front of the stove.

As I crawl in bed next to my husband, ole Story-ma appears again, this time in guise of an old man; she thinks she can trick me, but I have had much to do with her ways and she no longer fools me now: I know her smell – pimento and wood smoke and chocolate tea. The long white beard which hangs from the old man's chin is the same-same one which hung from her crotch; and I see how his balls swing low between his legs – two little pouches of brown magic. Quickly, I switch on the bedside lamp. *Share mi yu wisdom*, I write on my palm. Old Grand takes my hand in his and reads it, traces the ink with a tamarind finger.

"Gather your words, and don't give up," he says. "Watch the snail, she knows how. She is not the swiftest of women, but she hears a voice and circles the kitchen, leaves her story shiny-shiny behind her."

Ole Story-ma disappears and I lie awake watching the sky, wondering what star might fall. Later, I awake to a story smell curled up beside me – this time, a little baby, not quite three months old. She looks like any other infant except for one thing – long gray hairs grow from her tiny ears. Story-ma coos and kicks me in the side. In the dark, I fumble for my pen, but can't find it. Finally, I whisper into her ear, *Tell mi one more secret, one more time*.

"Turn your story over and over your woman tongue," she says. "Then, just at the right moment, when it's about to burst, pop it quick like a dark plum in your mouth."

Story-ma rolls over on her side, and I lie beside her listening to her soft breath go in and out. I want to get up and find my pen, but I am so tired now, so tired, and tomorrow there are the lunch boxes to fix and the clothes to wash and the dinner to cook and the floor to clean and the baby to hush, the baby to hush, the baby to hush.

My eyelids fold as my mind says "Wait a bit" and I am just about to drift asleep, when I awake, my heart beating fast, Story-ma falling from the bed, her little arms grasping air, her mouth open in fright, her head hitting the hard tile floor. I leap to her side, listening for her breath, holding her face in my palms. Just when I think little ma is dead, she opens her eyes and snarls, baring a row of small brown teeth.

In the yellow light of the kitchen, my pen races, dark ink circles the concrete walls. The words rush around and around, swirling the kitchen like wood smoke over bread-fruit. All night I work, crissing and crossing my heart and my tongue.

In the morning when the house awakes, I sit calmly at the kitchen table, sipping a cup of chocolate tea. "Look the shell, Mama," my daughter says, pointing to the empty spiral resting on the windowsill. And only she, little child of mine, notices shiny words slithered across the walls and my shirt still soaked from my wet and glistening belly.

I read her my story, *It's late and I'm up sweeping the kitchen,* tracing the words with a sure finger. My breasts rattle - two full pouches of cowries, river stones and black ackee seeds. The hairs on my crotch grow just a little longer.

Common Conch Shell

August 19, 2001

Sister Story-ma has been turning up in this place and that and always wild and womanful, a pen tucked like a silver ornament in her hair. Someone saw her at a Kingston dance hall; her lips were guava wet and her bare shoulders glistened under the lights. She danced all night with a young artist who fell in love with the way she swirled music around her waist, tossed back her head of dark dreads, the whole room swaying to the metarhythm of her laughter. He wanted to see her again and again, to write her number on his palm, but she slipped outside and never returned.

Another time, she was picked up by a New York taxi driver. She settled herself into the back seat, took out her pen and began to write with fervor up and down the length of her legs. The taxi driver stared into the rear-view mirror as she wrote and wrote on the expanse of dark skin. This went on non-stop all through traffic. At Lenox Ave., she tucked her pen back into her hair, slammed the door like a period behind her, the long story legs disappearing in the crowd.

Weeks later, she was seen at Miami airport, a return ticket to Montego Bay folded in her pocket. At the security gate she beeped and beeped, had to empty her pockets, take off all her bangles; still, she beeped again and again, till finally, they called her aside to an office. The supervisors searched her under bright neon lights; made her drop her clothes to the ground as they read the story written up and down her long brown legs, over her belly and under each breast. The story was written zig-zag this way and that, so that before they could even get to the end of it, she had them bewitched, motionless against the wall. Story-ma slowly put her clothes back on, all the while looking them coolly in the eye. She gathered her things and flung her red scarf over her shoulder, stood straight as sugar cane and left through the revolving doors. Nobody even had a chance to read the rest of the story which circled the long column of her slender neck.

A few nights later, I'm out in the yard, hanging curtains on the line. My bare feet are cool on the damp grass, and I'm longing for the bedtime mango waiting for me on the kitchen table when I see her shadow dancing through the vine leaf pattern of wet curtains. I drop the clothes pegs and run for my pen, enclosed in a notebook in the laundry basket.

She motions to me, "Shhh," and points to her legs, all lit up with words in the moonshine. She lifts up her skirt and carefully pulls the skin off each leg, just as if it is a pair of sheer stockings. Underneath there is new skin – smooth and poreless and waiting. She hands me the skins and says, "Put them on." I know from experience not to disobey her, but still I protest: "My legs not long like yours."

"Shush!" she whispers, and I quickly pull the sheer skins onto my legs, the words stretching around my knees, over my thighs. With legs like these, I could seduce hurricanes, change the course of rivers and rename the seven seas. I could . . .

Just before I begin to feel too beautiful, she snatches her skins away from me, scaling the fence and disappearing into the dark. All night I keep vigil by an open window. I want her words. I want her words.

In my early morning dream, I am driving in the back of a New York taxi. The taxi driver eyes me through the rear-view mirror as he chews on a matchstick at the corner of his mouth. He is tired and doesn't want any trouble. A little wooden cross dangles from his mirror, a picture of Jesus is glued to the dashboard. Our eyes meet and I wink at him as I pull my pen from behind my ear. When I reach out and stroke the bald circle at the back of his head, he tenses, but keeps on driving, weaving through the traffic. In red ink, I write around and around the smooth parchment of his skin, *and the word was made flesh; and the word was made flesh...*

The front door opens and I suck in my breath as Sister
Story-ma, drying her hands in the folds of her skirt, steps
into the yard. Her head is wrapped with three yards of red
cloth, and her dark eyes fringed all around with white
lashes are live anemones.

I am the woman who has been too long eating other
people's language; my tongue is withered, words shriv-
elled inside of me. I crouch under the ackee tree, gourd
rattle without seeds. Alva is calling, but I cannot answer.

Wood smoke rises from the kitchen out back, and Sister
steps forward, looks me over. She notices my red eyes,
the corns on my feet, the grey ash of my skin, my shallow
breathing. Wind rustles tamarind leaves, barble dove
feathers and frangipani blossom against the zinc roof.
Sister reaches into the string pouch around her waist,
pinches a little arrowroot between her fingers, then dusts
my tongue with the white powder before putting her pen
behind my ear. Goats bleat in the gully below. My nipples
harden; my cheeks sting. I run like cane fire, testifying
and cursing, prophesying and talking dirty, words flying
behind me all the way to the sea.

Under the ackee tree, Sister spits in the dust, takes a
stick and draws a circle around it, laughs, then goes back
in the house.

October 17, 2001: Meeting Alva

I have identified the ingredients in Alva's tears: pimento
and wisdom weed soaked in white rum. For weeks, I keep
Sister's pen in a box under the bed. I am afraid of it;
scared of what I might write; scared of the sparks which

might fall on the white over-proof rum, bursting Alva into
flames. One day because I am tired of ironing and because the house is quiet, I take it out and write, "Alva,"
on a clean sheet of paper. I sit at the kitchen table
mulling the name over, wondering to whom it really
belongs. I try making a doll in Alva's likeness, piecing it
together from sticks and bits of bark. I put it away – it
looks too much like me.

It is not until the following week that we meet by
chance – Alva Donovan, dark and high cheek-boned and in
her late thirties. That morning, I awake from sleep with
an urge to visit my grandmother's grave. Against my
husband's advice, I jump in the car and head across town.
When I arrive, Alva is standing by the cemetery gate; I
know right away that she is the woman with the story to
tell – those eyes about to spill over, the shopping bag held
so close to her side.

The cemetery is overgrown with macca and love bush
and the caretaker will not let us in. "Is late and not even
duppy safe in here," he calls. Alva looks off in the distance, a bit of coral vine caught in her hair. I watch as
she walks off and climbs into a bus; and I follow it all the
way to Papine where she gets out and rests on the steps
of a betting shop piazza. Her canvas shoes are torn and I
can tell her feet hurt.

I park and sit down beside her, my pen behind my ear;
both of us watching the soldier ants on the ground. When
I see that she is about to leave, I have to think quick – I
say, "Lady, you want to exchange your shoes for mine?"
She looks into my eyes as if they are a window straight
through to the other side and I take off my sandals,
setting them between us. She blinks – her lids like two
dark moths – before picking them up, and I know that my
shoes are more real than me. I am the dream and she is
the dreamer, but how alike our feet are! The dusty dark

skin, the bunion on the left foot, the sole arched at the same angle. She puts on my sandals, a perfect fit, and does not look back.

Likewise, I wear hers home, the insides printed with the name, Alva, in black letters. I leave the car and walk in the shoes all the way back – thirty years to where her story begins – a little girl in a gully throwing stones.

This then, is Alva's story as it was given to me over the course of three years.

Flamingo Tongue

Kingston, Jamaica

PART ONE

THREE RIVER STONES

Place your Alva doll on a windowsill facing east. Feed her honey and almonds and coconut jelly. Tie a red ribbon around your pen. Do not lift your hand from the page; do not pause to slap the mosquito on your neck. Write until her eyes flood with tears.

I

Evenings, they threw stones into the gully bottom – one stone for each memory. The person who threw the most stones won, the score scratched on the bark of a woman tongue tree. Usually the winner was Alva. She knew how to mix memory with imagination so that it didn't matter which was which. See her hurling a gray stone, her hair parted in the middle, brown sugar on her cheeks:

I, Alva, would not be wearing this skirt with the torn hem if the cloth did not catch on a nail sticking from the side of the house; and the nail would not have been sticking from the side of the house if hurricane Lloyd did not blow the verandah apart. And hurricane Lloyd would not have come at all if two women out on a fishing boat did not quarrel, stirring the wind and the sea to madness. And the two women – Eunice and her daughter-in-law, Lily – would not have quarrel in the first place if Lily did not rub down Ross Man (Eunice's son) with oil-of-compliance while he was sleeping; Eunice chasing Lily in the name of Jesus with a kitchen knife, Lily running and hiding at the bottom of the fishing boat. The thing is, Lily never would have found the boat if Mama did not call out to Daddy, just as he was about to haul it in from the beach; and Mama never would have call at all if Mildred's baby did not choke on a fish bone; Daddy rushing toward Mama's scream.

21

That day, Mildred's baby coughed up the bone and smiled, and the fish in the sea all kept on swimming. They were kin to the same fish which swam around the cargo ship which had brought Mrs. Ying from China and the sea was the same sea which smells of broken water and bears witness to all stories, real and imagined.

Tinge your ink with rosemary and god-bush. Write the boy doll's name at the top of the page. Burn the midnight oil.

Made in China

I, Made in China, would not be eating this tamarind ball if Nana had not plant the tamarind tree on the day I was born; and I would not have been born on that same day, March 5, if Mama had not fall from the stool in front the formica cabinet bringing on her labor; and Mama would not have been standing on the stool in the first place if she wasn't looking for the shilling hide beneath the bowl with the yellow flowers paint on it. And Mama would not have even need the shilling if she didn't craven for something sweet – longing for the coconut drops in Mrs. Ying's showcase. And Mrs. Ying's shop would not have been build at all if Mrs. Ying had not poison her husband and come to Jamaica on a cargo ship; and the cargo ship would not have dock in our harbor had the Caribbean sea not been there – waiting like the water ready to break from Mama's womb.

This is how the brother traced himself to China and back again; and this is how they came to call him Made in China. Years later, when Mrs. Ying hung herself from a tamarind tree, it made sense: Made in China's story had come full circle like a black bird flying above their heads. Sometimes, that is how stories are.

Meeting Made in China

Woman-me with two hibiscus blossoms hanging from my ears, see a boy walking down the street, bouncing his ball.

23

"Psst," I say, "What yu name?"

I am standing under a poinciana tree – my skin and dress dark same like wood. At first the boy don't see me, but then he makes out my yellow teeth.

"Paul," he answers, "but them call me Made in China."

I call him closer with my index finger. "Come over here," I say, opening the folds of my skirt, "Come and walk inside this little story"; and as I spread the skirt out wide, the boy sees that it is painted with a picture of the road ahead of him, just as it is right at the moment – the two leaning coconut trees, the bougainvillea bush hanging over the zinc fence, the bus stop on the corner with the girl waiting beside it, reading her book. Perhaps it seems to Made in China that there is nothing to lose, the painting on my skirt is exactly the same as his way home, it even changes as the scene changes – the girl at the corner turning her page as two black birds land on an electric pole.

Made in China finds himself moving a little closer to my sugar smell and he rests his head on my warm belly as I close the folds of my skirt around him. "Such a nice boy," I say, and he keeps on walking, bouncing the ball right through the story skirt, the girl turning another page of the fluttering book.

F.T.

February 1, 2002

Tonight I'm writing in the kitchen. No one, not even Girl, smells the wisdom weed rum except me. Coopie, my husband, says it's just my imagination. He don't know it, but tonight I proved him wrong. The wet sponge in the kitchen sink stunk of Alva and I squeezed a little into a

24

cup and tasted it, poured the rest into a lamp and lit the wick. It burned bright as morning star!

Sister says I should explain to Coopie the "nation" in imagination. What Sister says is true, but for now, I'm keeping the lamp a secret, writing all night by its flame.

F.T.

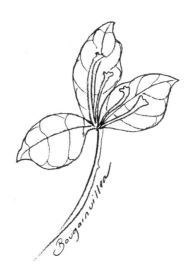

Bougainvillea

Arrange your sewing-machine-turned-writing-desk with a bowl of water, a dry coconut and a jar filled with Joseph Coat croton. Ignore the smell of rum on the tablecloth. Wipe Alva's tears as you softly call her name.

II

Alva, hair parted down the middle, working for the Catholic nuns – raking the poinciana leaves in the yard, feeding St. Peter on the verandah, setting the table as long as the last supper. At four o'clock the bell rings for evening prayer and the sisters disappear into the dark chapel, Alva changing the station on the radio, St. Peter eating red pepper from her hand, Marley swelling the neck strings of his guitar.

Alva, knowing too much. She once walked in on one of the nuns, Carmen Innocencia, in the bathroom; Carmen was naked, holding a mirror between her legs and clipping the dandelions in bloom there. Alva, her two plaits like lizard tails, knew where to find the bottle of white rum hidden behind the washroom and what time of month the sisters all bled together like a herd.

On the day that St. Peter decided to speak, "Babylon, Babylon," – every hour on the hour – Alva was given two weeks' pay, a loaf of bread, a quarter pound of cheese, three orange sodas and sent away. On the way out, she took the cedarwood Madonna from the foyer of the chapel, slipping it into her school bag. It was her little sister Dahlia's birthday and Alva wrapped the Madonna in pretty paper and wrote her name on it.

Later, this is what Dahlia remembers: the Madonna eighteen inches high, her face full, her mouth perfect as a guava leaf. She rubbed her dark skin with brown shoe polish and dabbed khus-khus perfume in her open palms. The Donovans were hand-clapping, speaking-in-tongues Pentecostals and their god was a jealous god, but Dahlia could not have loved the Madonna more had she been a Catholic girl in a large house in Stony Hill (for the Catholics they knew were hardly ever like them) with orange blossoms blowing across the tile floor and doctor birds and wind chimes in the garden. Her cedar arms stretched wide, the Madonna was tall and big-boned like women on Mama's side, the points of her crown sticking up like little plaits; and Dahlia knew her knees, if she could have seen them, would be large and fleshy like theirs.

Alva slipping bubble gum from the glass jar on Mrs. Ying's counter into her school bag, a fly pitching at the nape of her neck; it was the cedarwood Madonna who taught Alva how to be a pickpocket. Bored in the dim light of the chapel, her arms stiff, the cedar Mary willed sinners to pause in front of her, their hairpins and silver earrings falling at her feet. Cedar Mary chose little metal things because of the sound they made when they touched the ground – the tinkle so pure it made her insides shiver, God stroking her with His long finger, the baby Jesus released and swimming inside her. Alva swept up the little metal things at the end of the day, Cedar Mary's shiver a secret between them.

Alva, picking pockets just because she can – like grab bag, never knowing. A baby's pacifier. A stick of chewing gum. Two dutty kerchiefs. A fifty-dollar bill wrapped in banana leaf. She tears the chewing gum in two – half for Dahlia and half for Made in China – then sticks the money into her hair. Alva's hair holds all sorts of things – love notes, dried flowers, lotto tickets. At the end of the day, she brushes it all out, bits of this and that floating to the floor; Mama poking her head through the beaded curtain.

Mama. See her clear-clear – standing in the front door-way as she threads a needle, the needle for mending the torn hem of Alva's skirt. It is five o'clock and there are a few minutes to spare while the rice boils. She holds the eye to evening light and moistens the blue thread between her lips. The thread nudges at the eye but does not go through. Out in the yard, a mosquito skims the dust and waits for the back of Mama's knee as down the road a door slams. Soon the children will all come home, their school bags swinging against their backs; there are flies on the avocado; the plantains need more oil. As the rice boils over, the needle falls from Mama's hand, Cedar Mary biting her lip on the windowsill. Everything there is to know can find in the needle eye.

Three times Mama tried to hem Alva's skirt and three times she lost her needle; later Alva swept up just as she did in the chapel, dropping her findings into a small wooden box full of safety pins and paperclips, hair slides and little silver crosses. The secret to knowing was to watch the Madonna's shadow, her face in profile against the wall.

Daddy (Clive) – standing in the front doorway, opening a bottle of beer, his head tipped back, an apple dancing in his throat; the Madonna's mouth parted, the bottle stop-per falling falling to the ground, her neck jerking back in the moment the metal touches tile. To gaze directly at Cedar Mary would be to see only her half smile, her eyes focused cool-cool somewhere behind you. "God kissing her foot-bottom," Alva said. Alva knew too much – she even knew God's business.

Each day the Alva doll cries a small vial of tears; nights I leave the container next to her and by morning it is full. After I fix breakfast, I rub a little on my skin and save the rest for the lamp. The whole time I write, my daughter,

Girl, watching me. She is three years old and already knows how to spell her name. Her eyes watch my hand move back and forth across the page.

"I telling all Alva life," I say, and she smiles.

Later, she will feed the Alva doll parched corn and brown sugar from her hand-middle. I will know when the doll is not hungry anymore, words falling from the page soft as ground nutmeg.

Girl knows all my secrets. She saw how I stuffed Dahlia with salt and red pepper and she knows about the bees between Alva's legs, the needle down the length of Mrs. Donovan's throat. "Why Mummy?" she asks, and I worry about the story scaring her little red heart.

Outside in the yard, Sister is chewing on a piece of sugar cane. She spits the trash into a bowl then taps three times on the kitchen window. I send Girl to her father and go open the back door. It's raining softly and Sister smiles, her mouth full of teeth marked pretty-pretty with words. I want to see what the teeth read, but the letters are too small. "Take this," she says and hands me a piece of broken bottle-glass. She smiles again, and this time the words come into focus, *wax from a young child's ear*. Later, while Girl sleeping, I take wax from her left ear, smear it on a spoon and leave it on the kitchen sill.

All night I am thankful for quietness, sweet over-ripe mango, the mystery of ginger lilies in a jar on the table. Alva's tears fill the lamp and I write in the light of its dancing flame.

F.T.

Alva's favorite color is yellow. She likes hard dough bread with callaloo and salt-fish and her lucky number is 11. I am 6 months older than Alva. She was born at winter solstice and I was born at summer solstice. We met on the day of a partial solar eclipse visible only from New Zealand.

When I made her soul doll, I stuffed the belly with pink frangipani blossoms because those are her favorite flowers. I also placed a feather from a pea dove in the belly, though I'm not sure why. Lately, two pea doves have been visiting the yard. Girl loves the song they sing; even right now-self, she hums along with them as she swings.

Na na na naaa/

F.T.

February 3, 2002

So far, the kitchen is the best place to write. I knead the flour dumpling, jot down a word here, drop the dumpling in hot oil, jot another line or two there. I have all the dolls – one for each character – lined up on a shelf and Sister says to feed them often. Dahlia likes brown sugar but Made in China prefers limes sprinkled with salt. Alva is the one who surprises me. Each day she grows fatter and fatter. Mornings, I put the callaloo and saltfish in a bowl at her feet and by midday it has disappeared. The more I write, the more she eats. Coopie watches from the corner of his eye. He has grown quiet and distant. This story is costing too much.

F.T.

So I come across Dahlia on a bus headed for Spanish
Town. From my eye-corner, I watch her with her maga-
zine, circling pictures of women with hoop earrings. I
open my notebook, drawing in the margins – bananas and
guavas and lop-sided bowls. When the pregnant woman
behind me burps, I write the word "burp" coming out of a
bowl. When the boy on my next side says "Babylon," I
write that too, coming out of another bowl. All the way
down Mandela Highway, I fill the page with bowl and
word. Finally Dahlia starts to hum and it's a tune I know
well, *Three Little Birds*, and a bowl in the corner cracks
wide open.

F.T.

III

Daddy was a beekeeper. He had several hives in different locations – four in the Chinese cemetery, three in May Pen cemetery and five in the abandoned lot next to their house. Carefully chosen, the sites were all places which most people avoided so that the bee houses were really known to few, Daddy the artful squatter, selling honey in the market. The children called it duppy honey because the bees fed only on the nectar of pink coral vine and only if the vine grew near the dead.

Next door, the coral grew right over the spot where the neighbor, Isaiah, died – the bees captured from swarms in the hollow of the stinking-toe tree under which he was found. Isaiah had been a funny long-legged dread. He taught them how to make sailing boats from soda cans and little baskets from bits of wire. For nine nights after his passing, the bees danced, the children watching from under the stinking-toe. On the last evening, Alva wore her hair wrapped in a yellow scarf, a cotton blouse stopped just above her navel and three bead bracelets jingled around her wrist. As soon as she entered the yard, the bees flew to her in one swoop, covering her bare arms, burrowing into her chest; Alva stretching out on the ground and closing her eyes as if she had been expecting them all along, bees filling her ears, the hollow of her navel, the palms of her hands, every fold of her garment. She opened her mouth and invited them in, her knees swaying back and forth with pleasure and not one of the Donovans moved forward, for it was clear then who she really was. She rose up unscathed – her skin moist and shiny – and, without a word, walked back home. The whole family knew that Alva was queen.

Why Isaiah's bees chose Alva remained a mystery. The truth is, it was *she* who chose them – her power was clear. Men, young and old, longed for Alva's small round belly, but not one of them could have her. She lured with her honey skin and cowrie teeth but, in the end, gave herself only to the honey bees. Dahlia and Made in China had seen it themselves – Alva at the bottom of the gully with Gordon, the broom-maker's son. Alva, smiling then lifting her skirt to reveal her crotch, a swarm of bees.

It was through Cedar Mary that both Alva and Dahlia discovered their woman's temple. The temple from which they could shake down all God's little metal things from the sky; the source of their tallawah, the power to make things happen – the same will used to ride storms, stop dogs in their tracks, catch bullets and throw them back, make something out of nothing.

Dahlia was there when they stoned Alva. Her sister was walking past a bar with her shopping bag slung over her arm, when Gordon threw the first stone. It hit her right on the tail bone and she dropped her bag and swung around in disbelief; three bees flew out of her bosom. If the three bees had not appeared, perhaps that would have been the end of it, but as she turned to run, two more appeared and then someone else threw a stone and there were bees everywhere. They stoned Alva – Gordon and his two women friends – turned from their own power and afraid of hers. The evening *Star* called it a bar fight; there was a photo of a small bruised girl. Someone took Alva to the hospital and worker bees followed the vehicle all the way. They had to use chemicals to get them to leave.

Later, the bees found her head-tie snagged to a barbed

wire fence; they kept vigil all through the first night, but by the time Alva was released, they had found another queen. She came home in a taxi with bandages over one eye, Mama supporting her at the elbow. Daddy stretched her out on the red vinyl couch and Made in China took off her flip flops; she fell asleep curled up in a ball and stayed there for three days, her chest wheezing like a box with an insect trapped inside. At night Dahlia sang little made-up songs, *Come back, Alva*, into her open mouth; then flattened her ear against the board wall, listening to the parents' secrets on the other side – Mama blaming it all on herself for having children when she was past the age; Daddy remembering the bee which stung Mama behind the ear when she was pregnant. On the third evening, Alva sat up, scratching her scalp. She scratched and scratched, her hair like wild fern until a tiny key fell out, rolling onto her lap. "*That's* what I been looking for," she said, and Mama immediately went to the kitchen and boiled water, filling the bath with sinkle bible and bay leaves; Alva soaking her body in the tub, wings of dead bees floating around her.

Alva had lost an eye but not her spirit. She made a patch for the sunken socket and gained a new reputation as the one-eye girl. Mama and Daddy called her "that crazy Alva", and "slack Alva", but even as they said those words, they were loving her. Alva knew how to wear an eye patch so that everyone envied her; she made having one eye new and stylish. Children saw her on the street and longed for half sight, wondering what she dreamed of behind her decorated eye. Ah, to always have one eye closed, a secret door to dream behind; one eye looking, the other dreaming; two worlds unfolding at the same time.

Always a few steps ahead of everyone, the Donovans' small world could not contain Alva. Behind her secret door, she dreamed herself in New York, crossing the street in a red tank top and slim jeans, her cheekbones set at an angle to catch the sun. She got a job in a clothing shop uptown and weaved her way through traffic at Half Way Tree practicing the walk, bus drivers calling out to the pretty one-eye girl, Dahlia and Made in China eager for the treasures to be brought home in her hair.

It was round about this time that Mama began to wonder about the falling needles. Once, after she lost another one, she held out her hands and saw that they were shaking, and said half to herself and half to Daddy, "My fingers so weak, I can hardly hold as much as a needle." Dahlia wanted to tell Mama the truth of it all, but Alva said, no. They hid Cedar Mary under the couch but it didn't make a difference; the needles kept falling. Mama went to the doctor, but they could find nothing wrong. She drank bush tea to strengthen her nerves, but things remained the same. Someone told her to eat susumba, but that didn't work either. One day she stood in the open doorway and on impulse turned to look at Cedar Mary smiling her little I-didn't-do-a-thing smile. Dahlia and Alva were sitting at the kitchen table shelling peanuts. Cedar Mary's eyes were focused somewhere past the dusty shaft of light coming through the curtains; it was quiet in the house. Mama looked at her daughters; the daughters looked at their mother; no one said a word, but Mama knew.

Mama did not raise her voice (she was not one for raising her voice); she did not question Alva (she was tired of questioning Alva); she simply said three words, "Take it back." Alva did not argue; she wrapped Cedar Mary in a towel and put her in a shopping bag and went straight to the convent. Dahlia was the one who cried out, "No, Mama!" but Alva was already gone. She opened the gate without knocking; it was evening and the nuns were all at dinner. St. Peter was swinging in his cage on the verandah. As soon as he saw her coming he began, *Babylon, Babylon.* Alva gave him a little red pepper, put Cedar Mary back in place in the foyer of the chapel and then slipped out behind the washroom and left. Mama met her at the door and put the empty shopping bag in the garbage. She soaked the towel used to wrap the Madonna in bleach then spread it out to dry in the sun. Daddy was kept out of it.

Dahlia was almost eleven then and Cedar Mary had become so much more than the doll she used to be; she missed her. They were quiet at dinner, Dahlia and Alva. Made in China kept playing with his food, forming the calalloo and saltfish into a little volcano. When his fork fell, they all turned, out of habit, to look at the windowsill. And there was the Madonna – all smiles, her head thrown back at the usual angle, her eyes looking right through them.

Returning Cedar Mary turned out to be impossible. She was part of the household now and wanted to stay, each attempt to take her back resulting in her reappearance. Between the two of them – Cedar Mary and Alva – the house was full; Mama grew nervous and lost weight while Alva grew round and more womanly. Her hair became thick and springy; she had a high sweet smell like ripe julie mango.

The deaconesses were called in to bless the house; white shoes, white dresses, heads wrapped in white cloth, they went from room to room, praying out loud, one arm held to the bosom, the other raised in supplication; Mama Milly rocking back and forth, her eyes shut tight. Someone rubbed olive oil on her forehead and the women formed a circle around her, laying their hands on her shoulders. Dahlia remembers it well, Mama lifting her head, level with Cedar Mary's, her eyes widening, her finger pointing like a flame.

"But I know her," Mama said and everyone turned to look at the figure on the windowsill.

"Is Willa."

"Come now, Sister Donovan."

"Is she that."

"Come now, Sister."

"But look."

"No, Sister D."

Deaconess Ray broke into prayer, Mama Milly whispering, "Glory, glory," over and over. They tightened the circle around her; pressing her down, Milly curling into a ball. Afterwards, they all filed out of the yard, humming.

That week, Mama wrote a letter to her sister, Esther, in Brooklyn and joined the long line at the American embassy. It took eighteen months for the papers to come through and three more to scrape together a ticket. Alva packed her clothes in an old cardboard suitcase and Mama roasted breadfruit and fried fish to send for Auntie. At the airport Alva's one good eye was filled with tears, but in the other she was already wearing her red tank top, a canvas bag slung over her shoulder, prancing down Amsterdam Avenue with her long legs. They watched her from the waving gallery, Dahlia and Mama and Made in China; as she turned and blew kisses with both hands, she already seemed American. Dahlia and Made in China jumped up and down waving their arms while Milly turned away to hide her wet face, Alva entering the narrow door.

Alva sent them pictures from New York, her hair dyed the color of ripe paw-paw and worn in little chinee bumps, her eyebrows shaved to a pencil thin line. She worked in a garment factory and registered for night classes to get a high school diploma. She made friends easily, telling stories about her father's honey bees. The Americans laughed but then grew silent when they saw the yellow and black insects at the bottom of their glasses.

In the fabric stores, she asked for swatches of material – strips of velvet and satin, raffia and organdy to be made into patches for the missing eye. The patches were a fashion statement that only Alva could make – one had a mirror sewn in its center, another had a beaded psychedelic eye; there were eye-patches with embroidery, photographs and lucky charms; and Dahlia's favorite had the words, "kiss me," stitched at the bottom. Someone put her photograph in a local newspaper.

"My little girl with the torn hem," Mama Milly said, and she stuck the photos around the mirror; Alva watching with her dreaming eye.

Dahlia's bed was a cot in a corner of the living room, and one night when she should have been asleep, Mama came out in her nightie and opened the front door. It was hot and she stood in the doorway, sipping a glass of rum, the straps of the nightie fallen below her shoulders, the ice cubes lit up in the half light. She stayed there for a while leaning against the doorpost, fingering her earring, looking out into the street; it was late but when at last she moved, Dahlia was sure she had seen her take the silver knob from her ear, dropping it with what seemed like full intent. Because it was dark, she could not see the Madonna's shadow, but she did see her mother turn to look at Mary and smile. This is how Milly befriended Cedar Mary and this is how she stopped her needles from being stolen.

Next morning when Dahlia awoke, Mama was already dressed, standing in the doorway with her cup of coffee. Dahlia crawled out of bed and stood beside her; Mama squeezing her against her warm belly. In the kitchen Dahlia took the cornmeal porridge left in a pot on the stove, pouring it into a porcelain bowl with yellow flowers on the side, the same bowl under which Mama had searched for a shilling when she slipped and fell and brought on her labor twelve years before. As she grated a little nutmeg over the porridge, Dahlia watched her mother set the coffee mug down on the windowsill then hold a No. 6 needle eye to eye with Alva headed south on the A

38

train, the door sliding open at Penn Station; Mama moistening the blue thread between her lips, then pulling it through with one sweep of her hand; Alva stepping onto the crowded platform, red and yellow beads clicking around her wrist.

Under the ackee tree in the yard, Mama fixed the torn hem of Alva's dress; tiny stitches all the way around, she drew in a breath after each one, the cloth thin and worn – dots and spirals against a blue background.

Concerning Mama (Milly Donovan)

I met Mrs. Donovan through the eye of her needle. I should have known it would be so - I come from three generations of seamstresses and have always felt that pen and needle are kin, one stitch at a time like one word at a time. It was easy, then, to understand Milly - her stitches small and careful like syllables and half syllables across a page.

After my encounters with Dahlia and Made in China, I wrote nothing for several days; then one evening as I stood in the front doorway with my pen behind my ear, I noticed a woman knocking at the gate with a stone.

"Please, I'm begging you a piece of blue thread," she called out. I am used to people begging at the gate. The week before, a girl asked for a cool drink of water. I brought out a jug on a tray printed with a map of the West Indies and she drank it down - "Thank you M'am" - crushing the ice between her teeth. Over the years, people have asked for money, food, work, but never thread. This was new and my response surprised me: I simply held up my sleeve and tugged at a thread

unraveled at the seam. I pulled and pulled and watched
the thin blue yarn trickle to the floor onto the blank
paper of my open notebook, forming a pattern of horizon-
tal lines, one after the other down the length of the page.
Out by the gate, Mrs. Donovan was holding up a No. 6
needle.

"Come on in," I called. "Open the latch and don't mind
the dog."

Concerning Clive Donovan

Mr. Donovan sold me a bottle of honey from his stall along
Red Hills Road. Business was slow and he was grateful for
the company; I got into conversation about tropical
flowers, the flight paths of honey bees and how to cut
down a wild nest. I did not tell him that I knew all about
his family.

"So how come the bees don't sting you?"
"Smoke."
"What kinda smoke?"

* * *

Mr. Donovan's trick for making honey:

1. Check the trays often.
2. Scrape the trays with a hot knife to expose the honey.
3. Comb the honey-filled holes and drain.
4. Strain and store in old rum bottles.
5. Ignore the fact that there is something funny going on
   in your house.
6. Ignore the fact that certain bees are in love with your
   daughter.
7. Ignore the fact that there is a Catholic Madonna on the

windowsill of your house, you, whose daddy was a Pentecost minister and whose god is a jealous god, visiting the iniquity of the fathers upon the children unto the third and fourth generation.

8. Stiffen your neck and take care of the bees.

<u>Cure for a common cold</u>:

Honey and white rum and lime.

Writing into the middle of the night, I spread Mr. Donovan's honey onto hard-dough bread. My sticky fingers smudge the page. I write and write my way through wood smoke till finally, I find one sentence which stings.

In the midst of all this, I have another surprise - letters from Carmen Innocencia, a junior sister at the Catholic Convent. How she caught wind of my writing, I will never know. For several months, the letters come steadily, each one written with a fine-tipped pen on onion-skin paper. The handwriting sprawls across the page in jumps and leaps, and I think to myself, this is a woman with something to clear from her chest.

F.T.

November 22, 2001

Dear Ms. Woman:

Last night as I reach for the water on my night stand, I notice that it tinge with blue. Good thing I had turn on the lamp, or else I would have put it straight to my lips. I lay there with my back against the pillow, watching the water darken bluer and bluer; and even anansi as I am, it took me a while to realize it was ink from your pen. So, I see that you mean to get under my skin, my secrets seeping from the tip of your paper mate. I know your kind – writing is a cover for necromancy. But do you really think you can take on Carmen Shane, me, aka, Sister Innocencia who once stole a man's breath while his body rode mine?

While my tongue is loose, you might as well know too that I was there, watching from a window above the shop when you sat with Alva outside the betting shop piazza and exchanged your shoes for hers. I saw how your foot-bottom resembled hers and how you walked away wearing her sandals. But what do you think Alva is doing, Ms. Woman, while you are lost in neva neva yard writing in her tear-up shoes? And what, I'm wondering, will she discover waiting at the gate of the cemetery wearing yours? Ah, there are at least two sides to every story, but do you really want to tell both?

Later,
Carmen Sister Innocencia Shane

December 21, 2001

Dear Ms. Woman,

This morning I saw it again, bits of blue ink crusted up at the corners of my eyes. Who do you think you are? And just who gave you the right to poke at my sleep?

Carmen Sister Innocencia Shane

January 4, 2002

Dear Ms. Tongue,

You are a trouble maker, but believe me, you have met your match and whether you like it or not, I plan to use your pen to have my say. Here is a bargain: change my identity in your little book and I will tell all, my white habit blooming like queen-of-the-night blossom.

Carmen Sister Innocencia Shane

January 6, 2002

Dear Flamingo Tongue,

I had a feeling you would not resist. Attached is a statement of non-disclosure. Please sign it and return promptly. Any published records of our communication should bear the new appellation, Carmen Sister Innocencia Shane.

Sincerely,
CSIS

January 8, 2002

Dear Writer-Ms.,

I received your inquiry about the room above the betting shop. It's a small space I rent from time to time when I get my one or two weeks leave. At such times, I take off the Church of Rome white and put my plain Carmen clothes back on; that way nobody pays me any notice as I sit and catch the breeze from the open window.

Not long ago, back when my skin was still spice and warm, I used to live in that same room. It had a single bed, a sink and a chimmy, and a bureau with a broken mirror; kitchen and bathroom were shared with a family in the building out back. I was nineteen and worked in the bar across the street; that's where I met Jukey, the man whose breath I would steal. Seven years later and still I return to that room, watching for the reappearance of a girl named Willa.

Willa was Jukey's only daughter. The day I took her father's breath, she was sitting across the street waiting for his return. She must have been about eight years old; I remember looking through the window and seeing her sitting on an upside down bucket, cradling a new doll. Her father told her not to move, but to wait right there – next to Brother Lloyd the street-corner evangelist – while he dashed over to the betting shop to watch his horse. Jukey entered the shop, slipped out the side door, then ran up the back stairs straight to me. I turned from the window just as Willa kissed her dolly on its forehead, Jukey's feet on the concrete steps. It was the day before Christmas and as he appeared in the doorway he seemed tired, his chest wheezing like air in a squeaky toy. He set two creme sodas and a bag of red and white holiday canes down on the bureau and we stood there rocking in each other's embrace, me with my face against his chest, one eye watching the girl waiting anxiously across the street. When he slipped his hands beneath my shoulder straps, my dress fell to the floor light as mango blossom, the curtains flapping at the open window.

We hadn't meant to remain long, there in each other's arms, but it had been three weeks since we last saw each other and the little girl was safe next to the preacher, down below the nylon curtains. I straddled my legs around Jukey, pulling him against me on the little cot, for though he had seemed tired and had forgotten the asthma medi-

45

cine, I didn't know that he would stop breathing, right there on top of me. All I remember is that he lunged forward in one smooth movement, arms tensed, eyes shut tight; his lips were maroon like bruised starapple and as I reached out to touch them, he pulled in a breath, **Carmen**, and how was I to understand the difference between death and ecstasy?

March 3, 2002

Dear Ms.

Years ago, I confessed to Father Rose that in my heat I took a man's breath. Father Rose listened quietly, masturbating behind the booth, his privates slick in his large hands.

CSIS

March 4, 2002

Dear Flamingo

I have heard of stories which balm like medicine, and I come to you in search of heart ease. If I tell you all my pain o heart, will you write a story like that?

CSIS

Jukey's wife worked at a bakery, watching the machine which sliced the bread; I imagined her cinnamon like his cinnamon daughter, coming home from work with flour on her hair, calling, "Jukey Jukey," and finding the daughter huddled in a corner holding the rubber baby. For days after his death, I stood outside the bakery watching for a big cinnamon woman with four thick plaits just like her daughter. On the day I saw her, I was surprised at how beautiful she was, two fierce eyes sunken in a chiselled face. She held a plastic bag with bread-ends and I pictured Jukey kissing her small wrists with his starapple mouth; and I wanted her to have him back, to see her hold his head against her belly, to hear him say, Mona my Mona.

The nurse in the ambulance covered Jukey with a stained sheet and only after they left did I realize my nakedness, my dress unbuttoned, exposing my breasts. A small crowd had gathered to watch the scene; there was silence for a moment and then Brother Lloyd raised a chorus. A robust woman, head wrapped in cloth, joined in shaking her calabash, and as the onlookers dispersed, I remembered Willa. I ran down the road calling out her name, asking for the little girl with the four plaits curled up at the ends, but no one, not even Brother Lloyd had seen where she disappeared. It would be a whole year before I saw her again. She returned twelve months to the day and to the same spot, holding her rubber dolly.

CSIS

April 10, 2002

Yes, the day Jukey died, he promised Willa a Christmas present. I heard her little voice through the open window, "Is what, Daddy?" her ribbons bright in the December sun.

"Someting silver," he called crossing the street, and I saw how her face broke into a smile. That afternoon as I tossed Jukey's pants across the floor, two silver bangles fell from his pockets.

April 17, 2002

Even now as I eat the body of Christ, I still hear that jingle of metal on tile, the little girl waiting next to the preacher man, the baby in her arms turning flesh.

April 18, 2002

She returned then, one year later – December 24, 1993. I was standing on the steps of the betting shop when I saw her cradling her baby doll wrapped in blankets. She looked left and right, rocking the baby from side to side. The street was in motion with higglers and children and plastic toys; Willa standing there on the curb, puffy crescents under her eyes. She hummed a strange aria which rose up with Marley on the juke box, catching the attention of people in the street; I stood on the steps watching fruit flies hover around her head, my tongue heavy in my mouth, unable to call her name.

Jukey's cinnamon daughter returned every year and each time my pain o heart grew heavier. She filled out with breasts and put on weight and soon it became clear that she was too old to be playing with dolly. Still, every Christmas, she seated herself down on the curbside, hushing her baby and humming her little tune. In her cotton dress and flip-flops, she looked like any young mother holding her child and waiting for the bus, but every now and then someone peering over her shoulder, noticed that the baby did not move, the rubber forehead exposed beneath the blanket.

Someone named her "Christmas Card Girl," and word such as it is, got around, people pausing to watch her close her eyes and hum. Year after year, the curious were quiet and even reverent as Christmas Card Girl stirred them to fullness with her cornmeal-sprinkled-with-cinnamon voice. Then too, because it was the season of blessings and because they wanted to please the Madonna, people dropped pennies into the diaper bag at her feet. She held the boy child warm against her breast, her voice rising up in little gusts and only I knew that she was really there to wait for her Daddy and the silver present he promised to give.

The last time she appeared was in 1999. She was sixteen years old and had the same bruised look under her eyes; I had been waiting all year for her arrival, her voice stopping me mid-motion as I swept up bottle caps in the bar.

It was Dago Man, the Rasta with the withered leg, who carved her from a bit of cedar wood. He studied her from his seat on the betting shop piazza, taking it all in – her lips pushed out like peppers, her hair sticking up, her eyes large with prayer. It took him nine hours to complete his work, the whole time a matchstick in the corner of his mouth. I bought him a water coconut and a piece of bun with cheese and as I watched over his shoulder, wood shavings covering the ground, I saw it myself – the Cedar Mary's little smile as his keys fell to the ground.

April 29, 2002

Record of items found in the foyer of Sacred Heart:
23 hair pins
3 silver earrings
1 silver plated chain
1 shoe buckle
1 cuff link
30 safety pins
5 straight pins
1 padlock (small)

1 key
1 key ring
2 rings
3 silver buttons
52 needles
2 silver crosses
1 tooth filling
Forty dollars and fifty-five cents in silver coins
1 zipper clasp
1 silver minute hand from a Timex wrist watch
18 paper clips
3 small screws
1 metal door knob

May 1, 2002

Dago Man gave me the carving in exchange for cleaning his room and washing his clothes. I shined his floors with red polish and a coconut brush, dusted all the tables and wiped down the louver windows. While I waited for his clothes to soak in the tin basin, I scrubbed his pots under the stand-pipe in the yard. I was folding the last of the shirts when he returned; the staff used to support the withered leg gave him the silhouette of a man twice his age. He sat under the almond tree smoking a spliff and watching me gather the clothes pins. He had a faraway look in his eye. Afterwards, he wrapped the Madonna in brown paper, placing her in my arms, "Take care of her, hear?"

That night, the Madonna put me to the test, but saved my life. A woman came into the bar crying and cussing and searching for her baby father. Her man was somewhere in the bar drinking out the baby milk money, she was sure of it. She searched high and low, pushing her way to the restroom, and when she couldn't find him, she took a lighter from her pocket and held it to the coconut straw partition. Someone shouted, "Bloodfire!" and I saw her synthetic hair go up in flames, the room immediately filling with smoke, the bamboo lining the ceiling all ablaze. I rushed for the back door but remembering the Madonna in a bag under the counter, turned back. Part of the ceiling crashed down, flames lapping rum on the floor, blocking the back exit. Had I continued to the back, I would not have made it.

I escaped from the fire but the woman searching for her baby father did not. For weeks, I smelled her synthetic hair, her baby's wails disturbing my sleep. The bar was badly damaged and I was out of work; I took to the streets with enough change for bus fare and the Madonna in a brown paper bag; that's how she led me to Sacred Heart.

May 24, 2002

I never did find out what happened to Willa. Dago finished his carving and blew the dust from its face; when I looked up the girl had vanished.

May 31, 2002

All I know is, the edge of the world is a betting shop in Papine. Horses sometimes leap there, and so do men and women. Nobody knows where they disappear after that, but I think they end up in a place swirling with stars, cinnamon and brown sugar; yellow cornmeal sprinkling their skin. A man with four plaits curled up at the ends, meets them halfway; he kisses their foot-bottom with his starapple mouth. I would like to go to that place.

Carmen

Note:
The more I think about Willa, the more I know that she is the girl I used to sit next to in Mrs. Murdock's grade 3. She used to carry a baby doll to class every day in her school bag and she fed it tamarind balls and grater cake at recess. She had moons on her fingernails which she said she stole from the sky at night when God wasn't looking. I remember lying in bed and dreaming of the star I would take from God, just like Willa. I would place it on my tongue, light exploding sweet and sour in my mouth.

The last letter from Carmen sister was more of a warning. It was scrawled on the back of a prayer card and folded into a No. 10 envelope.

F.T.

June 7, 2002

Careful how you wear another woman's shoes.

CSIS

Alva's shoes are the plastic flip-flop kind. I walk in them until my feet hurt, but to write her well, I know I must find a way to inhabit her skin. As I sit writing in the kitchen, Story-witch laughs over my shoulder, the kind of laugh that leaves me wondering whether I am pleasing her or just making a fool of myself.

"Give mi Alva's skin! Let mi put it on," I say.

"Too dangerous," she whispers and as she leaves, the back door swings shut.

PART TWO

WAX FROM A YOUNG CHILD'S EAR

Be a stone for a day. Sit by the side of the road. People might think you mad, but be still. Listen to the ground beneath you; your back, a resting place for a lizard's belly.

I

With Alva gone, Dahlia and Made in China had to find new ways to amuse themselves. That was the summer they made a big sister in Alva's likeness – One-eye Girl. One-eye Girl called out to them from her place among rocks. She went, "See me here! Yu don't see me?" They ran their fingers over a red boulder and felt the little mound in front of which was One-eye Girl's belly; they saw that one side jutted out to the left like a little arm, and that a dark circle marked the place where her breasts would grow. Down in the gully, another smooth rock was already breathing, damp as skin. They carried it up to the yard where it balanced perfectly on One-eye Girl's shoulders. Mama watched from the kitchen window where she grated nutmeg over two enamel mugs of condensed milk. They drank it down, marveling at One-eye Girl's small brown navel.

They were ten and thirteen, but as Mama said, already old. It was election time again and everyone was a little on edge; four years before, they had watched through holes in the zinc fence as a man stabbed Isaiah in the chest, the machete rushing into the spot where he kept a pocket full of cool blue mints. Isaiah pushed his cart around town selling snow cones and ice cream. One afternoon, he drank too much white rum, arguing politics with a stranger outside the betting shop. It was too late when he realized that the man had a forked tongue and scales on his neck instead of skin. He followed Isaiah home and left him sprawled beneath the stinking-toe tree, his eyes sealed koala nuts. Afterwards, Dahlia and Made in China leaned against the back wall in silence, peeling bits of paint like scabs from the house.

One-eye Girl stayed all summer. They filled the cupped hand at the end of her outstretched arm with rice and made a bead necklace for her throat. With colored pencils they gave her small half-smiling lips and one enormous eye that would never close on them. She watched the yard all around in four directions and when they played hide and seek, she was the one who knew where to find them. In the evening, they sat in the dust and leaned against her belly as they listened to the radio and cleaned the rice for Mama's pot. One-eye Girl was warm and solid against their backs. They were safe with her. Every morning she smiled at them, her skin moist and speckled red, and at night they watched through the window as the moon bathed her blue and grass-quits settled the length of her arm. They knew of no one more beautiful.

October came and for Dahlia's birthday Daddy bought her bun and cheese and creme soda; they ate it out in the yard, watching two barble doves pick at the crumbs. After the sky turned indigo, Made in China lit two white candles, wedging them onto One-eye Girl's shoulder. They flickered side by side, tall as the number eleven and Mama said, "Look how you turn my good bleaching stone into graven image," her voice like faraway wind blowing curtains on a clothes line. They all sat on the back steps watching the candle drip warm milk onto One-eye Girl's chest. Two dogs barked, and down in the gully a little gust blew hair from someone's comb, a broken shoe lace, a few bottle caps, a chain of silver clothes pins. Cedar Mary smiled from the open window.

The next day, no one was particularly anxious when the radio warned of a tropical storm. Such warnings were common, and usually amounted to a bit of lightning and a few claps of thunder. With no clouds around for miles, the sky was a still glass of water. Nevertheless, Clive climbed onto the roof to secure the zinc and they picked the last of the ackee from the tree and drove the hens inside the coop. The radio said the storm had already passed over Cuba and was gathering strength, headed straight towards them. All afternoon, Milly stood in the doorway watching the horizon as the breeze from the electric fan on the coffee table flapped at her skirt, fanning the yellow cotton to life like little flicks of light. Later, though there was still no rain, a wind came up from over the Blue Mountains, the air filled with something electric.

That night, all the rain in heaven would not have quelled the start of the election riots. It was around twelve that the street broke into ruckus. Dahlia and Made in China listened as a group of boys threw stones, breaking the windows of the apartment above the Chinese grocery shop. Mrs. Ying's scream, like shards of glass, spun down the gully, waking the dogs and silencing the crickets. Clive took out his machete from under the bed, sending the children to their room. Soon afterwards when two men with guns broke into the yard, both children scrambled through the back window and crawled under the house. The men pushed the front door open as if they owned it, turned out all the drawers with Milly's medicine and loose change, shook out her large-print bible, a pressed hibiscus falling to the ground. As they ransacked the living room, Dahlia and Made in China crouched underneath the house, watching everything from a crack in the board floor. The men fought the machete from Clive's grasp and tied his hands behind his back. Milly stood directly above the children, a hole in her nylon stockings; they kept their eyes riveted to their mother's exposed heel as one of the men held a gun to her neck. The wind grew stronger and they clung to each other, their mouths open; a glass of water fell from a side table and Milly began praying, her words rushing over them. They shot Clive first and Milly broke into tongues. There was silence and then there were two more shots.

Dahlia and Made in China listened as the men ran down the steps and out into the yard. One of them circled the house, while the other paused to look at One-eye Girl. She looked straight back at him, the half-smile turned wicked, her raised arm commanding him to leave. The moon was out and One-eye Girl was dressed in blue again, a lizard stretching itself in the middle of her palm, fireflies hovering about her head. The man stepped back, laughed a small uncertain laugh, then called to his comrade who had just knelt down by the side of the house.

They could see them clearly now; they were men in their twenties; one of them was shaved bald and the other, tall and lean, wore a dark stocking scarf. What happened next can be understood in different ways, depending on who you ask – Made in China or Dahlia. Made in China says that the two got into an argument, the tall one picking up One-eye Girl's head and throwing it at the other before they ran from the yard. But what Dahlia remembers is One-eye Girl's eye closing and then opening. The lid was shut for only a moment but she remembers how it fluttered like a wing, and how when she opened it, the eye suddenly brightened before it turned again to stone. It was then that in his astonishment the tall man picked up the head and flung it across the yard. In that instant, Dahlia's tears ran hot down her cheeks; the top of her head opening and bursting into flames; she could have scalded the men with the sheer heat of her blood. It is this opening, this surge of power which for years, sustained her like fuel.

After the men took off through the dark of the gully, Dahlia and Made in China dashed into the house where blood splattered the white linoleum, the glass table top and the plastic passion flowers. Clive was crouched in a corner, his head fallen between his knees; Milly was sprawled on the kitchen floor in a pool of red. Her hair pulled back with a rubber band, she seemed younger and girlish. Her lips were smeared with the guava she had been eating right before the men broke in and she had one hand clenched across her chest. As she opened her mother's fist, Dahlia saw how small the hands, hushed doctor birds. The fingers parted, releasing a spray of yellow fireflies, and there in the sudden light, the kitchen shone in the eye of the storm.

Later, when the police were gone, Dahlia and Made in China took One-eye Girl's head back down to the bottom of the gully where they had found it. She had already given them everything that she could give.

Through the Eye of The Needle; or What Milly Told Me:

Milly's request for blue thread came a week after I made her soul doll. Her pupils were all dilated as if she had stared into the eye of her needle and seen sorrow-self.

"One word at a time," I said.

"One stitch at a time," she answered.

Needle and pen are twin and this is a story of Alva and her twin sister, Willa. This is the story of how Milly carried her two babies to town to buy a half pound of flour, a little salt-fish, a head of yam; and how she missed the bus and evening catch her on the road; and how she stand up by the curbside, the two babies bawling, the shopping bag digging into the skin on her shoulder; and how she never like that part of the road because even though it full of people it have plenty lonesome bird and sometime if you don't careful the lonesome bird, them start up conversation with you.

It was the day before Christmas and the time was busy; Milly stand up watching the road for a ride and that's when she see one of the birds on an electric pole. It had a thread in its mouth and it fly down a little lower and pitch on the fence behind her. The two babies were in a basket at her feet, because that's how she usually carried them. She heard the bird break out in song and she so mesmerized by the song that she turn around to look, the voice so much like a woman humming to a child. Milly watched the little brown bird, its eyes shiny, the thread still in its mouth. When she turned around again one of the babies, Willa, was gone.

The police station was down the road and she headed there right away. Someone called Clive at work in the re-upholstery shop and they searched all evening and for several days. Some people said it was obeah. Some people said it was the lonesome bird. Other people said, no, that's foolishness – someone in the crowd must have taken the baby while Milly wasn't looking. The police said, "How unfortunate." Some people said every before-Christmas one baby in the corporate area get snatch and the good-for-nothing authorities ought to look into it. The police said, "There is no conclusive evidence." Somebody wrote a letter to the *Daily Gleaner*. Someone wrote a song about it. Milly cried every time she heard the song; Clive rubbed her tired feet and fed her noni and irish moss.

She went to a balm yard and had her body stretched and washed for seven days in rum, god bush, leaf-of-life and search-mi-heart. Balm mother said, "Write Willa name and give it to her twin-half, Alva, to swallow. When the child come of age and the time ripe, watch story come around, your two daughters together in this same street."

F.T.

Miss Mary dead,
a who
kill him?

All day the pea dove out in the yard singing this song.
She pecks at dust,
watches from under the lime tree,
leaves a brown feather on the back step.

Where is her nest?

Leaf of Life

Discover the Donovan's ancestors. Read through your notes then rewrite them in reverse, following the story backwards. When you arrive at the beginning, keep on writing, your hand gliding across the page, tracing navel-string back to first mother.

II

Because there was nowhere else to go, the children went to live in the cemetery. They found a corner away from the road, over-run with love bush and coral vine. The cemetery was not unfamiliar to them – they had spent many hours with Clive attending to the bees there and now it was the home of two new graves marked with sticks.

The dead welcomed them, as no one else had, the ground bearing dandelion, jumbilee and yellow cerassee fruit. Dahlia and Made in China were not the only tenants to the dead; they gathered material for shelter, learning from a family of five living on the opposite side by the west gate. They found pieces of board blown down in the gully and cardboard boxes behind the supermarket. One rainy night, they stole a tarpaulin from a truck, throwing it over the cardboard roof then securing it with rocks. The dead did not complain.

Both of them made friends with children over by the west gate. There were two their age, Arlene and Bobbie, plus a baby, Blue, because of his color at birth – like midnight, his mother said, and his eyes two yellow moons, each with a dark hole in the middle. For a long time, they continued Clive's honey. He had taught them how to cut wild nests and they knew all about the scraping, combing and straining into rum bottles. They went around collecting the bottles behind bars and betting shops and when that didn't work, they looked for empty syrup or guava jelly jars in people's garbage. They washed them in public restrooms, collected the honey and sold it in the market. A sold bottle or two could buy a loaf of bread, an orange soda or a water coconut. Dahlia and Made in China shared the honey with Melva, the mother at the west gate, and in return she looked out for them – washing their clothes in the gully, cornrowing Dahlia's hair.

Honey collecting was hard work and left little time for romping on the tombstones with Arlene and Bobbie. They went to bed exhausted, seeking comfort in the presence of the bees or the light of a few fireflies caught in a jar. Except for Alva stitching lapels and pockets in the garment factory abroad, they were alone in the world. They became friends of the dead, invisible to the living. The fireflies blinked on and off and they both imagined Alva somewhere in New York, all those tall buildings like teeth in an open mouth. How easy to be lost there, falling into some dark crevice, swallowed by the great tongue of the earth. They fell asleep, their heads to the dirt, listening to the ground hum.

December came and Dahlia and Made in China were reminded of Cedar Mary buried alive under a poui tree for safekeeping. They argued about whether they should sell her in the craft market where she could easily bring them money for two beef patties, bus fare and a bar of soap. In the end, they left her in her shallow hole, covered with dirt and dry leaves.

For Christmas, Melva gave them packets of chalk, taken from a teacher's desk at the primary school where she sold tamarind balls in the yard. They marked hopscotch on the tombstones with Arlene and Bobbie and when they got tired of that, Made in China came up with the idea of a treasure hunt, drawing arrows and picture clues on the graves. In this way, they spent the better half of a day transforming the cemetery into a treasure map, the boys working on one side and Dahlia and Arlene on the other. Coming up with treasure worth hunting for at all was not easy, but both Dahlia and Made in China had learned well from Alva and immediately thought of Mrs. Ying's shop. First Dahlia walked by to make sure there were no customers and then at just the right moment, she stepped in, holding up a cup.

"Please I'm begging you a little ice," she said.

Mrs. Ying looked her over, then turned her back to open the cooler.

"Next time, I charge you," she said over her shoulder; and Dahlia reached for two of the coconut cakes on the far side of the counter.

Later, she broke off a corner of one of the cakes, leaving it on Mama's unmarked grave, then wrapped the rest in newspaper, burying it for treasure.

For one whole day, they were all children again, hunting from one headstone to another, Blue following behind and chewing on the end of a stick. Dahlia remembers Blue well – dressed in a little red T-shirt, his bottom conveniently bare for peeing on the graves, his legs spindly like river sticks, his belly a round calabash. He ran behind them, trying to keep up and pointing to the black birds swirling above, Dahlia and Arlene singing as they skipped among the tombstones. *Six yellow bananas happy to be alive, a bird eat one and dat left five. Five yellow bananas hear a bird caw...*

Dahlia was the one who heard Blue cry out – a small yelp like an injured puppy – but when she turned around, he was not there. She and Arlene had to walk some yards back before they found him, fallen down into a freshly dug grave. The children all tore out running into the road then, calling for help, but it was too late. A crowd gathered in from the street and someone turned Blue over with a stick, exposing his face; his eyes open and resting on a bird pecking at dust.

Made in China said it was all his fault for coming up with the treasure hunt in the first place. But someone in the crowd blamed it on the woman for whom the grave had been dug; they said she had died giving birth in Kingston Hospital, her baby's navel string tied around its neck. She had come now for the dead baby and mistaken Blue for hers. Then too, one must not forget the birds from someone's rooftop in New Jersey which, only the week before, all rose up, flapping their wings as a girl flung open a window to call out to a taxi waiting in the street, the birds heading south a day early, wings spread to catch the wind, following the curve of the Hudson and then on down, through Virginia, South Carolina and the long leg of Florida, the Caribbean all aglitter, Blue lifting his head to watch them chatter above, his little feet slipping into the hole. All this is true, but just like the memory of stones, if you chase fault back far enough, it disappears every time – into the sea as salt.

To this day, people still see Blue running through the cemetery, a bright streak of light the color of his name, stealing flowers from all the new graves. Ask Melva. She knows. Nights she waited in the cemetery with a basin of water to catch the shadow of her duppy baby, Blue flitting around and teasing, his laughter soft as dragonfly wings. "Blue! Blue!" but he was off to the other side, a flash against someone's headstone.

After the incident of Blue's broken neck, a reporter began sniffing around and taking photos. Later Dahlia and Made in China saw it themselves – Melva's clothesline in the evening paper, strung out from pole to lime tree and still holding Blue's diapers. Another article a few weeks later carried photos of the honeybees. The squatters were not happy for the attention and soon after there was talk about relocating them to a landfill on the other side of town.

It was in the midst of this that one afternoon the children saw a woman stepping around the graves, making her way towards them through a haze of fruit flies, pushing back coral vine and love bush. Her head was tied with a red cloth and she seemed to be an ordinary woman, like someone's auntie or mama, except for one thing: as she stood in front of them and opened her mouth, they saw a dark mark on the tip of her tongue.

"You still have honey?" she asked, but she hardly gave them a chance to answer, so full of talk she was, going on about the price of honey, and her goddaughter called Honey, and how to mix honey and rum and lime and the meaning of a bee in a baby's bath water; so that Dahlia and Made in China heard only half of what she said, so taken they were by the mark on her tongue, so intent on trying to figure its shape, but she kept on talking, her mouth working like a wheel, how to tell a wasp different from a bee, and how milk and honey good for ulcer stomach, and how King Solomon fed honey to his concubines and how many times the word honey appears in the Bible but kiss mi rass, don't yu know there's no such thing as the land of milk and honey. At this she let out a laugh, tilting back her head and exposing her tongue, the dark mark like an X on its tip.

"Them call me Bad Rice," she said; and they both stood there for a while staring at Bad Rice.

Bad Rice came every week for a year. She said she was using her ten percent tithe to buy honey instead because Pastor was a thief who spend the congregation money on satellite dish and a new fence for his yard. Always she came with a loaf of bread, a can of condensed milk and a clove of garlic which they were told to swallow. She gave them an address: 311 Hayden Avenue, Kingston 11, where they could receive letters and that is how they kept in contact with Alva. Alva had by then over-extended her three months visa and was an illegal immigrant, still living with Auntie Esther who was in and out of hospital for kidney failure. Whenever she could, Alva sent American money – ten dollars, twenty dollars – carefully folded and stuck between a card. Bad Rice took it to the bank and changed it for the children into Jamaican currency. Made in China's favorite was the bill with Sam Sharpe on it. He believed that if Daddy Sharpe could make it from slavery to a fifty dollar bill (though not worth much) then he could find a way to make it out of the cemetery.

Bad Rice did not like talking about herself and was careful to never let anything slip about her life at home (which they assumed was 311 Hayden Avenue.) She said she had spent time in jail and was given the name, Bad Rice, for not knowing her place. She was born with things to clear off her chest, she said, and could not help it, her mouth got her in trouble.

It was Bad Rice who got rid of the newspaper man when next he came around. She stretched her body across the door, preventing him from pushing his way into the children's shanty; and when he took out his camera, she let loose her tongue, reeling a string of words which sliced the air like a machete, sending the newspaper man, his arms held up in surrender, straight through the gate. Dahlia and Made in China were Bad Rice's charge and she would guard them anyway she could.

The first week of January came and Bad Rice appeared again, dragging a bag of exercise books, pencils, a blue tunic for Dahlia and a khaki suit for Made in China.

"Free paper burn," she said and put them on the bus, sending them off to school. Bad Rice waited for them at the cemetery gate every morning for a month, seeing to it that they caught the bus. They were happy for school – there we toilets there and sometimes toilet paper and, best of all, there was lunch served warm on enamel plates along with a cup of powdered milk. Mornings, they dressed quickly and ran to the gate, eager to see Bad Rice, glad that they were a part of something.

In letters, they told Alva all about Bad Rice and she wrote back saying how pleased she was, but adding that they should keep guard, because "don't she sound little bit strange?" Alva had failed the exam for the high school diploma and was still working in the garment factory. She said the manager paid her "under the table", and for a long time, Dahlia pictured Alva crouched under a counter, pretending to look for fallen needles, the manager discreetly sliding a white envelope underneath, Alva crawling out when the coast was clear. With things not going well for Alva, the children clung even closer to Bad Rice, so fearful they were that they would be left alone.

***

"Bad Rice, is where yu really live?"
"Where I live is none of yu rass business."
"Bad Rice, why yu talk so?"
"Yu don't see how mi tongue mark with an X?"

Concerning Bad Rice

Finding information on Bad Rice was not easy. The Hayden Avenue address she had given Dahlia and Made in China did not exist, and after much searching, the only record of her name was found in a place I did not expect – on a headstone dated 1958 and which meant she would have been dead for many years when Dahlia and Made in China saw her walking toward them in the cemetery, a swarm of fruit flies about her head. Someone had decorated the grave with sea shells and it was surrounded by several empty bottles, their necks stuck into the ground. The stone read, "Marion Tate Rice a.k.a. Bad Rice, departed 1958" but there was no birth date. Learning her full name gave me another starting point for my research; I spoke with other Rices on the island, contacted the Registrar General in Twickenham Park, went through stacks at the Jamaica Archives, but still, I came up with nothing. For all I know, she could have just walked out of the sea one day and taken up residence on the island. I did find out, however, that there is a family connection between the Rices and the Donovans in Jamaica. Could Bad Rice be a relative, one of the old guardians? In the end, in the little pin cushion of my heart, I knew that Bad Rice wanted her past kept secret, and I have decided to honor that.

Meanwhile the Alva doll so fat and so hungry I have difficulty keeping up with her. Every day she craves something new; this morning – rice porridge sweetened with condensed milk. The odor of her tears still fills the house. I am disturbed, but perhaps I should not be – I have read of this condition. Wessalworth first recorded it in his 1789 *Journal of the West Indies* – a slave boy separated from his mother and experiencing extreme sorrow cried tears which upon closer examination proved to be alcohol of the highest degree. Similar cases were reported of men and women under the whip and especially of women in labor. To my knowledge, there has been no such occurrence in modern times.

Sister visits less frequently now. Still, sometimes I hear a cough or a sigh and I know it is she by the window, the breeze shifting the cotton curtains ever so slightly.

Coopie says I am losing weight, the Alva doll getting fatter and me getting more mawga, just like Millie Donovan. "She sucking you down to skin and bone," he says.

I think Coopie is even a little afraid of me. He sleeps in the extra room off the verandah and flips through my notebook when I am not looking, sniffing the pages and holding them up to light.

What he really expects to find?

F.T.

Take a piece of red chalk and draw a picture of a door on the wall. Decorate the door with photographs, feathers, leaves, old letters, bits of broken crockery, stones, coral, newspaper headings, seeds, rags, bone. Give the door an elaborate handle. Walk through it.

III

The cemetery was a crossroads for the living and the dead and sometimes, it was difficult to tell which was which. There were people like Mrs. Grant who came every week with croton leaves and a bottle of white rum, sprinkling it all around her mother's grave before putting the bottle to her mouth, swishing the rum around, then spitting it out. Mrs. Grant visited like clockwork, spitting rum to stop her mother's duppy from meddling in her business.

Then there was the old rasta they called Guitar Man who came with his praise songs for the dead, *much respect for bring I this music*. He sat on the graves, picking out tunes and tapping his foot, white smoke curling above his head, and the children could not help feeling that sometimes he sang for them as well, urging them on. After he left, they scoured the ground and if they were lucky, found a half-smoked spliff which they lit up and passed between them.

One evening, Melva was scratching dandruff from Dahlia's hair when she heard what sounded like Guitar Man's voice howling over the radio. Melva turned the sound up higher and everyone stopped and gathered close; it was him. Guitar Man had made it to the airwaves and they could hardly contain themselves; it was as if they were privy to the very voice of God speaking light into darkness. That night Made in China dreamed of Guitar Man and in his dream every pore of his skin was accounted for and numbered, the sum of all things so clear and spread out before him, Guitar Man nodding and whispering, Seen?

Made in China often contemplated this dream as he wandered among the headstones, trying to make sense of things. That night, huddled around Melva's radio, was the first and last time they ever heard Guitar's recording. Later, they called the station, but the dj claimed to have never heard of it and didn't seem to know what or who they were talking about; Guitar Man, oddly enough, never returned to the cemetery. Bad Rice said, "Him pay him respect and gone."

My communication with Sister Innocentia has led to the understanding that Guitar Man and Dago Man – the artist who carved Cedar Mary – are one and the same. After Innocentia recounted the story of Cedar Mary's genesis, I went in search of the old rasta. Tracking down Dago Man was not easy. He had moved from his Kingston address and no one living in the yard remembered him or knew of his whereabouts. My only lead came from an old woman who said she used to cook Ital for him. She said he had people in Lucea and a sister in Brown's Town. I decided to go with the Lucea lead first.

It took me about a week, but eventually I found Dago Man outside his one-room house on a stretch of road between Harvey River and Johnson Town. It was a colorful red, green and yellow place, with the words *House of Zion* painted above the entrance. He sat in the doorway eating a mango; his locks had turned gray and were tied together with a piece of string; his eyes had that same faraway look Carmen described in her letters.

Interviewing him was a challenge. A man of few words,

he was contemplative, his gaze often lost in the thicket of bamboo and fern across the road. Steeped in scripture and dream, his words sometimes left me spinning. Here is an excerpt from that transcript:

Interview with Dago Man

F.T.: You remember a girl them did call "Christmas Card"?
DAGO: (Smile) Yeah man. Once I carve a daughter, I keep her in I system.
F.T.: What you remember bout her?
DAGO: The heap o plait them that curl up from her head like john crow vine.
....
F.T.: But is what else you did see in her that day?
DAGO: Let I-man put forward this reasoning: Mary come as a witness, same like how she did come with John to the tomb. I look at that daughter and wise-up situation.
....
F.T.: Dago Man, how it feel inside, deep inside, when you carving with your penknife?
DAGO: (Smile) It feel like House of Zion.
F.T.: Yeah?
DAGO: What I find now is that House of Zion is a place in the heart. Is in here (pointing to his chest). I love the work and work rise over I. Seen? I am under the work and the work is higher than I.

(Much respect to Dago Man for allowing me to conduct this interview. He passed away two weeks later on June 18, 2000. The House of Zion still stands.)

F.T.

IV

In the cemetery there were graves decorated with broken crockery, mirrors and shells. There were graves with bottles containing letters, bits of scripture and family photos. There were graves with food left on top – a dry coconut, a piece of wedding cake, a basket of cashew – which they dared not eat. But the grave which the children remember the most was the one with the bird's nest. A small brown bird with a watchful eye often sat in it, the nest made of grass, and what looked like human hair. They watched the bird for many weeks until, one day, it flew away, revealing a silver ring at the bottom of the nest. The grave was adjacent to Cedar Mary's burial spot and the children immediately suspected that the ring was her doing. Dahlia put it on her thumb and couldn't get it off and Melva said, "Mind duppy pin yu down and marry yu." Her fingers swelled around the ring, the skin turning itchy and discolored; she tried everything – soap, Vaseline – but it would not come off. For three days, she was married to a duppy. It was Bad Rice who finally said to "pee pee on it," and she did. Within an hour, the ring fell off, rolling onto the ground as if it had always been too big for her. That evening, Made in China dug up the box with the Madonna's shiny things, dropped it inside and then reburied it.

March 24, 2002

Last night while I was writing -

F.T.

Alva's Spoken Word Story #1

jump/pimento/fever/salt/riverbottom/zion/
chickenwire/bend/cane/watch/swips/sweet/live/gate/
see/book/bawl/bread/titty/shout/back-answer/burn/
long/shit

Words like these I stitch in the brims of hats, the
hems of shirts. Don't ask me why because I do it just to
pass the time. I hate this place. I write the words with
marker onto bits of ribbon and before work, I fill my
pockets-them. At the garment factory I sit at the
sewing machine, and every so often, slip one out, sliding
it into the fold of a hem.

White-heart/bread-fruit/alligator/cross/ital/hip/
January/lone

Don't bother ask me why – I find I must have to do
it, same like breathing; but who is to tell whether "coco-
plum" stitched into the hem of someone's shirt might
not change their luck? Mama used to tell the story of a
mother who gave her daughter a doll with the word
"sing" stitched into its throat. One day the girl took the
bus to Crossroads and as she got off there was a woman
down on the ground fighting her baby-father. The
woman held a ratchet knife to the man's throat and was
just about to stab him in the chest when the girl found
herself singing. Something about the girl's voice made
the woman pause. Unable to stop, the girl sang and sang,

77

the song filling her up, music falling soft as coconut flakes on the ground. The man forgotten now, the woman with the knife sat on the curbside with her face in her hands. Suddenly as it started, the song dried up in the girl's throat; she sat beside the woman and took the knife away. The woman's name was Velda and the voice in the girl's throat that day was the voice of Velda's long-dead mother singing as she tied a ribbon in her daughter's hair.

boat/tick/iron/moon/eat/table/hold/glass/feather/
wipe/banana/breeze/egg/
fan/shout/crotch/cow/duppy/balm/shut

The supervisor like to walk the aisles. He is a mawga bend-up man with dark goatee and little pawpaw seed eyes. Don't ask why I take the chance but just as he passes my machine, I slip in another word – rock/

Mama used to make our school uniforms and church dresses and take in sewing on the side. It was she-same who made Auntie Esther wedding dress. It took her two weeks of staying up late every night. I helped her sew on the beads and sequins and the mother-of-pearl buttons. It turned out Auntie Esther was pregnant and when she stopped by to try it on three weeks later the dress didn't fit. Mama had to pick it out and try to widen it. I remember all the stitches-them we pulled out, little bits of white thread falling to the tile floor. We had to pull them out careful-careful so as not to tear the taffeta and then Mama sewed lace panels into the sides of Auntie's dress. On the day of the wedding, everyone said Lord how beautiful the dress was and nobody knew that I did stitch the word, "fuzz box" into the new inside seam. I wished no ill on Auntie Esther and stitched it there for no reason other than the fact that I was ten years old and bored. I picked the word at random, by closing my eyes, opening a dictionary and running my finger down the page. "Fuzz box" sounded funny and so I wrote it out on a piece of toilet paper and sewed it to the seam of Auntie's dress.

On the day of her wedding Auntie Esther woke up with a scratchy throat. It was strange, she said, because she was otherwise fine. All day her voice sounded like someone with a kerchief tied over a phone receiver. At first I doubted the connection between my fuzz box and Auntie's voice but then I tried it again with different people and the same-same results.

kiss-teeth/ so-so/ limbo/ new/ blouse/and/ skirt/ and/ mongoose/ true

Don't bother ask me why don't bother ask me why don't bother ask me why.

Willa's Background Vocals (Bob on the Juke Box)

The tune in my throat like a long-long thread/

(As recorded from Carmen Innocencia's window)

Set a bowl of water at the feet of the soul doll. When you hear her sneeze, close your eyes and begin to write. Do not mind that you cannot see; do not mind that your words are not straight. Keep writing until the itch on her foot-bottom becomes yours.

V

The best thing about the cemetery was the poui tree and its yellow September flowers. The ground underneath was covered with soft grass and the children would lie underneath it and fall asleep. At school, teacher asked everyone to write a story, and Dahlia wrote hers about a beautiful poui tree in the middle of a cemetery and the lives of the two children who were comforted by its branches. Teacher had her stand up and read the story aloud in front of the whole class. Nobody knew that she had really written about herself – she and Made in China playing on the tombstones, searching people's garbage, going to the toilet in plastic bags then throwing the shit in the gully, rain water washing it away; both of them so tired under the poui tree, little leaves falling falling, camouflaging their asleep bodies.

After she finished, everyone clapped and teacher let her choose something to take home from the book box. She chose a book by Laura Ingalls Wilder because she liked the name "Wilder" and because she liked the grass bracing against the wind on the cover. She took the book back to the cemetery and sat under the poui tree, reading by yellow evening light and imagined Laura playing with her and Arlene, and she longed for blue ribbons and a wooden house by a river.

With school to think about, the bees were left on their

own, darting from blossom to blossom, busy about their own business. Alva wrote and said she had a dream in which she was trapped in an empty rum bottle. One night soon after they received her letter, vandals came and upset the hives, stealing six bottles of honey left on a tombstone. The cemetery was in fact, becoming increasingly unsafe. Overgrown with bush, people up to no good hid from the police there and one night they heard a woman's scream followed by the sound of breaking bottles. Early next morning when Dahlia and Made in China saw the police coming, they both turned and walked away, trying to be quick without drawing attention to themselves. A police-man met them by the gate; he asked where they lived and they answered 311 Hayden Avenue. He asked who they lived with and they answered Bad Rice. He laughed and said "Who dat?" and Made in China thought quick, "Wi god-mother." Lucky for them, they were dressed in school clothes and looked as if they might half-way belong some-where; the policeman let them go, warning them to stay away from the cemetery – "duppy racecourse", he called it – and they ran off down the road, not returning till evening.

It was teacher, Mrs. Parns, who in the end discovered their secret. Ever since the poui tree story, she took special interest, bringing books for Dahlia to read and lending maps for her social science project – a history of Jamaica's cemeteries. Maybe it was because Dahlia knew too much about the dead, or maybe it was because she smelled like them, but one day Mrs. Parns turned to her and said, "You don't have to stay there, Dahlia."

For all her good intentions, teacher scared the children; the last thing they wanted was separation. That afternoon they packed their things in two scandal bags and headed for 311 Hayden Avenue and Bad Rice. For two days they searched, taking their feet to the streets, tracing maps, questioning bus drivers, but 311 Hayden Avenue was nowhere to be found and neither was Bad Rice. On the third day, they retraced their steps to the cemetery where Kingston buttercups were in bloom among the empty beer bottles and cigarette butts. There was a drunkard talking to himself under the poui tree. They crawled beneath the blue of the stolen tarpaulin, the cardboard walls printed, *this side up.*

They came for them on a Wednesday – two women looking around and taking everything in. They were tidy and good-teethed and not unkind. They explained that they had been sent to take care of them, find them a proper home. Dahlia started to cry and one of them gave her a red and white mint. She took it from the woman and flung it across the tombstones, the top of her head opening and exploding like the night Mama and Daddy got shot. Made in China peeled off the clear plastic on his, placing it on his tongue, careful as a last rite.

He left with the fat lady with short, straightened hair and Dahlia went with the tall one with bifocals like two glass jars, each containing a dark fish. Dahlia watched as Made in China pressed his forehead against the car window, waving and making a monkey face. The monkey face was supposed to make her laugh, but she could not. She would not see him again for years.

Bad Rice was standing at the gate as they drove away. She seemed so small – almost transparent, her black dress with the red hibiscus print shifting in the breeze, vacant as a garment hung up to dry. When the children looked into her eyes, there was nobody there.

To this day, Dahlia hates mints. I know this because each time Girl leaves one at the Dahlia doll's feet, it falls to the ground.

F.T.

Alva's Spoken Word Story #2:

For years now, I dream the same dream – a woman with a pen behind her ear. Last night, I dream I see her again; this time sitting with her back against a coconut tree. She opened a little notebook and began to write and in the dream I was a small-little girl and I picked scab from my knee and ate it and pretended not to notice her. She was dressed in a so-so yellow dress and her hair was tied high with a red scarf. As always, I could not quite place her.

I watched her walk away, and as she left her scarf come unloose but she kept on walking, the red cloth unraveling and dragging on the ground. She left by the front gate without looking back and I ran after her down the road, gathering the cloth in my arms. I woke up, a bowl of rice porridge at my feet, a red thread caught in the fan by the window.

dub/belly/swirl/Jamaica/zinc/blue/guinep/tongue/girl/ dry-eye/ ginger/ sea-salt/stop/

Even now as I shake the kitchen mat, Alva's words stream through my head. In the American factory, the sewing machines tap up and down, stitching cotton underwear, Alva snipping stretchy nylon and pausing to gaze through the window, eye to eye with me facing north in the open doorway.

The more I think about her and Willa the more I see that the two resemble. Today I made a Willa doll and stuffed her belly with cornmeal and cinnamon. I bathed her in clear water then left her to dry out in the sun. Later, as I put a feather in her mouth, she began to hum. Right away, Coopie looked up from his newspaper and I quickly turned the radio louder so as to throw him off, Willa's voice joining in with Rita's on Marley's back-ground.

So, the seed Milly gave Alva to swallow has finally come of age. As Alva grows fatter with Willa's story, the pea doves in the yard become more and more restless. I know what Milly expects. Tonight I will feed the Willa doll rice and fried parrot fish; when she is full, I will write her words across her belly, the smooth cinnamon of her shoulders, the rise of her hips.

F.T.

Kingston Honey Bee

85

PART THREE

THE STORYBOOK YARD

I

The lady with the swimming fish took Dahlia to a house all the way in Portland. She said that a woman, Mrs. Shilling, had read about them in the papers and offered to take her in. Made in China was to stay at the orphanage in Kingston but would be found a home later. The fish-eye woman smiled with her good gapped teeth and Dahlia turned and watched the bird shit caked on the side window. They drove through the old zinc neighborhood, the gully stinking, and as they approached the former Donovan house, Dahlia saw that a girl was sitting on the steps eating guinep and that a woman stood in the front doorway, watching the world go by. The girl was her, she was sure, and the woman in the pink dress was Mama, and all of a sudden she was driving past her own life, and she wanted to scream and jump out of the car, but when she opened her mouth it was as if the guinep seed the girl at that moment spat into the air landed in her throat, lodging like a stone. This stone, this sadness, has never gone away. In moments of occasional pleasure she has forgotten it, but then later when all is quiet, it always returns.

That day, she fell asleep just as they crossed the parish line into St. Thomas, her dreaming full of the smell of rotting flowers. It was in this dream too, that she remembered that they had forgotten Cedar Mary, buried alive behind the cardboard shanty. In her dream, she wanted to get to her, to dig her up, but the dead smell was all around and she could not move through it.

When Dahlia awoke, Portland was green and thick with fern and mango and red hibiscus. A light rain was coming down misting everything, and Madda Shilling stood waiting by the gate, shading herself with a banana leaf. She was a short round woman in her sixties, her ankles swollen over her canvas slippers. She smelled of moss and damp earth and the day Dahlia arrived, her teeth had been sent away to be fixed, her lips collapsed inwards, her words spoken with a lisp. The teeth came back two weeks later, but they squeezed her gums and in spite of several more attempts by the dentist, they remained the same. The Madda Shilling Dahlia knew then would always be without bottom teeth, and it was her light lisp, tha tha tha tha, which greeted the young girl, softening everything, making the world right.

Dahlia walked toward her, her feet in wet grass, and Madda opened the front gate, slowly, like the cover of a storybook, the yard filled with flowers – croton, bachelor's button, monkey tail, angel's trumpet, Joseph's coat, hibiscus, ginger lily, anthurium and white and magenta and true-pink and nearly-pink and evening-time orange and soon-a-morning yellow and cross-mi-heart red bougainvillea. Two green lizards chased each other across the tile floor and Madda shooed them away, "Gail and Robert, enough!" with a swift motion of her hand. The lizards disappeared behind the potted ferns, an over-pink blossom falling to the floor.

Dahlia was almost thirteen years old, but as Madda held her hand, guiding her past the shrubs and potted plants, she felt like a small girl noticing the world for the first time. Madda led her to the back of the house where a room had been prepared with a cot and fresh clean sheets. A mahoe-wood bureau with an oval mirror and kerosene lamp stood in one corner, and on the far wall there was a calendar with a picture of an old-time map of Jamaica and the date of Dahlia's arrival, November 30, circled in blue ink. The side table next to the bed was covered with crochet and on top of that there was a saucer with a ripe Bombay mango; a jar of water on the windowsill held a yellow and red croton. As Dahlia took off her shoes, setting them aside, Madda fluffed the pillow and whispered to no one in particular, "Poor thing, she must tired." She left, leaving the door slightly ajar, her canvas slippers flip-flopping on the tile. Dahlia picked up the mango and smelled it, holding it to her nose as she stood looking through the open window, Madda outside now, scattering crushed corn to the chickens in the yard. Long after Madda went inside and closed the back door, Dahlia lay on the bed, the mango against her cheek.

In the morning Madda fried cornmeal dumplings and opened a can of mackerel and made chocolate tea. They ate heartily, Madda recounting her dream of wild hogs from the night before. In this dream, the hogs stole a man's Bible and buried it under tamarind leaves; and only after a hurricane named after his mother did he find it – a sow's hoof resting on the shepherd's psalm. Dahlia listened to Madda with interest, watching the way her nose quivered when she laughed and bit by bit in the morning light, her eyes awoke to Madda's skin – the little beetle on her chest, brown and almost imperceptible among freckles and spots; the fire-fly quiet and dark like a mole at her temple.

Later, after they fed the dogs and closed the doors, Dahlia oiled and twisted Madda's hair into little bumps, then left her facing the open window. It was then that the butterfly came, brushing against her bare shoulders, then spreading its wings – magnificent in gold and black – at the nape of her neck. Dahlia watched through a crack in the door as Madda fed the swallowtail sugar water from a bowl and she saw how it rubbed its feet together, Madda sitting on the side of the bed and watching the moon.

Sometimes I think Madda Shilling and Sister Story-ma must be two first cousins. Changing and fly-by-night as Sister is, I might never know. The Shillings in Portland go back to – but enough – Sister has reprimanded me that this is not about her.

F.T.

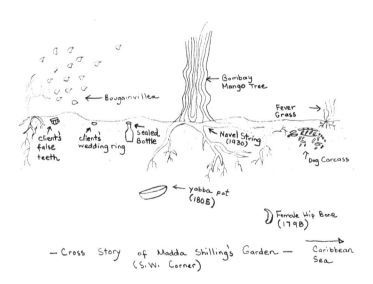

— Cross Story of Madda Shilling's Garden —
(S.W. Corner)

All July Dahlia worked with Madda out in the flowers yard, learning Jeremiah croton and bull-foot orchid, oleander and sleeping hibiscus, the hum of anthuriums. They watched the bamboo grow, examined the underside of rocks for worms and Madda pointed out rare snails by the side of the road. Madda had kept company with snails all her life and knew many of them to be tired women who come up with ways to take a break from the cooking and cleaning and all the things in the world which break their backs and their spirits. For every day in Jamaica there are women who can't take it any more; they hold up a long finger and say, "hold on deh," and then go outside and take a deep breath and sink all the way into a beautiful whorling shell which has been carefully hidden beneath their hair. Snail time is slow time because snails claim permission to just please themselves, one hasty minute to others, experienced as a whole hour to them. When snail women have had enough, they crawl out to the roadside and return to human self, take a deep breath, then walk back to the house to calm the children, or to finish the conversation with the husband left at the kitchen table, or to slip into the back pew to hear out the preacher and his foolishness.

This is why you see so many country women walking close to the edge of the road and why you should be careful as you swerve around corners. Next time you see a snail, watch it with new understanding. Notice any yellow and black spots spiralling around, coiling counterclockwise, turning back time. Make sure you don't look away to tie your shoelace because when you search again you will not find her; she will already be gone, disappeared among stones. Look for a piece of bark glistening with her trail; if you are patient, you might learn her language.

Madda reminded Dahlia that snailing is something to be learned and not a calling for just anyone. The last thing a woman needs is to be taken by predators like that woman who got trapped in a researcher's bottle and was carted off to a lab in Pennsylvania, her baby left crying in its crib. She ended up in a glass case in a university museum and in order to survive, went into hibernation, deep in the pink whorls of her spotted shell. Her family in Jamaica called the police, assuming she had been murdered or drowned in the Thomas River. She had been a sensible woman who loved her family and not one to just pick up and run. They formed search parties, scouring the whole of Brown's Town, her rubber slippers found on a rock by the river, but no sign of clothes or anything else.

It was a whole year before a research assistant at the university opened the case to clean the glass, giving snail woman a chance to crawl out and make her escape. As soon as he left the room, she transformed herself to human form and walked out the door. It was raining outside and she had no shoes. She stepped into the street and tried to remember her name, rain filling her mouth, her breasts suddenly heavy with milk. Suffice to say, in the United States the government is not too clever and you can bet they would be surprised if they knew how some immigrants really enter their country.

Jamaican snail women are usually of the following varieties:

1. "True Tulip" (white or pink shell with brown blotches)
2. "Common Nutmeg" (yellowish or cream shell with pale or dark brown spots)
3. "Common Dove Shell" (brown, white, orange, pink)
4. "Flamingo Tongue" (glossy, orange shell)

When the snail woman in Madda's story contacted her family in Clarendon, nobody believed her, nobody except the great grandmother, Nana Mae, who knew of such things and from time to time had been a snail herself. The story goes that Nana Mae regretted not taking time to teach her great grands; she thought the younger generation didn't know old-time business and figured that with all the nowadays fanciness like electricity and television it had all been diluted from the blood. But the blood is memory and, sooner or later, the heart which pumps recalls. If a snail woman had been trained properly, she would have stayed away from the path of possible danger, rested awhile on the spiral staircase of her mother-of-pearl, then returned in timely fashion to her baby waiting in the crib. Still, if it wasn't for Nana Mae, the family would have disowned the woman, so disbelieving they were. And even then, she and her husband went their separate ways.

<u>Willa's Background Vocals (Bob on the Juke Box)</u>

Think you're in heaven, but you living in hell/

(As recorded from Carmen Innocencia's window)

II

Made in China was never placed with a family. Dahlia and Madda Shilling were told that he ran away from the children's home, scaling the fence and disappearing into the street. Knowing that he had run in search of her, one morning Dahlia took the bus to Kingston instead of school. She wandered downtown looking in shop fronts, the market and all the usual places, then took a minibus to Mrs. Ying's grocery shop. There was a small crowd gathered outside and she could tell right away that something had happened. She heard a child crying and Mr. Ying shouting something in Chinese as he closed all the windows. She pushed her way through the crowd, climbing on top of a garbage can and from there she saw it all – Mrs. Ying hanging from the tamarind tree in her pink nightie, a bag of rice scattered at her feet. Her hair was loose and fallen about her face, her body dangling alongside the sour tamarind pods as black flies gathered at her lips.

A cat crawled onto the bag of rice and a woman in the crowd began to pray, "Deliverance! Deliverance!" By the time the police came the woman was speaking in tongues, the crowd turned church, swaying together, understanding every word of her fire language. They cut Mrs. Ying down from the tree with a machete, her nightgown catching and tearing on the branches, and Dahlia longed for Madda Shilling and her garden of a thousand flowers, the sanctuary of her zinc roof.

After they put the body in the ambulance, she made her way to the cemetery; it was dark then, the moon a thin slice, her socks catching on macca and bits of barbed wire. She soon discovered that their cardboard and zinc was gone, an old cheese-can the only evidence that she and Made in China had ever been there at all. She rubbed her foot across the ground, trying to find the spot where Cedar Mary was buried. She bent down on her knees, poking at the ground like a cat, but still could not find her; tired and hungry, she had been holding her pee since three o'clock, her bladder a balloon; she bent down to relieve herself and that's when she heard a laugh.

Dahlia turned to see a man waving and coming toward her; hardly able to stand, he appeared to be drunk. She pulled up her pants and ran in the direction of Melva's as fast as she could. He followed behind her, calling, "I coulda really love a duppy gal," and she threw her school bag in his path. He tripped and fell, shaking with belly laugh, his rum bottle breaking on someone's grave.

When Dahlia got to Melva's, there was nobody there; the place empty except for a pile of old clothes and an upside down bucket with a toothbrush on top. On an old blanket which she recognized as Blue's, there was a dog with a litter of nursing puppies. She crouched into a corner, concealing herself with the clothes, her eyes shut. The drunkard walked past, still laughing, and she sank against the dirt floor.

Dahlia awoke the next morning to the dogs still suckling their mother. In the blue gray of morning light, she walked the four corners of the cemetery calling Made in China by all his names, Paul, Paul Boy, Paul Boy Donovan. She wanted to see his best monkey face – cross-eyed, tongue touching the nose, lips stretched out at the two corners. She wanted to call back Daddy's bees, to gather all the stones they threw into the gully. But the cemetery was silent, and in the end, the only thing left to do was head downtown and take the bus home.

Once again, it was raining in Portland, and as if she had known the time of her arrival all along, Madda Shilling was right there, waiting for Dahlia by the side of the road, a banana leaf shading her head. They went into the house without saying a word. There was a bowl of cornmeal porridge waiting for Dahlia on the stove. It had been sweetened with brown sugar and condensed milk; there was nutmeg sprinkled on top. She drank it down and Madda Shilling cut two slices of hard dough bread, spreading them with butter. Dahlia had never had butter so yellow. All this passed without words, Madda Shilling moving about the kitchen, folding and refolding the kitchen towels. She made a cup of chocolate tea and Dahlia drank that down too before using the last of the bread to wipe the cornmeal from the bowl, and then, because she could not hold it in any longer, the tears came, the guinep seed lump in Dahlia's throat bursting open.

Angels'
Trumpet

Alva's Spoken Word Story #3

The supervisor walks by and I cut my eye at him. On the outside I am brave but on the inside I am crying. I hate this place. The eye-water gathers in little pockets under my lids. The supervisor passes again and I can't hold it in any longer; the eye-water comes down smelling of pimento and wisdom weed soaked in white rum. All afternoon I sew and I cry and I sew and I cry.

I want to reach the woman in my dream. I want to pull her by her red scarf...

Mrs. Ying Speaks

A boy come in the shop one day, maybe he eighteen or nineteen. Say his name Made in China; say he looking for his sister, Dahlia, like the flower, Dahlia. I think he making joke on me, "Made in China" bull shit, so I say, maybe your sister run away to China, those kind of flowers grow well there.

The boy start to cry, big boy standing there with tears on his face. That's when I think maybe I know him. I remember him; little boy who used to come in my shop with his sister. The girl, she steal from me when I turn my back. She think I don't know, but I always turn my back so she can steal. She take my paradise plums and grater cake; I push them close so she can fill her belly. After she leave I smile and watch her run down the road. I think they used to live in the cemetery. Sometimes I drive past and slow down and watch. I see their clothes on the line there, close to where my son bury.

So when I realize this, I make the boy sit down, wipe the tears from his face, give him a cup of water. Start at the beginning, I say. And he say when his mother pregnant, she craven for one of the coconut drops in my showcase.

It was evening and I close the shop and I take him in the back and give him a plate of meat and rice. He wipe the plate with his bread and say, Thanks. And I tell him about the cargo ship I come on, full of plastic slippers and wash basins and water guns and tea sets mark with his name. Someone hide me in a toilet, I say, and when they find me it too late to throw me out. I sail in that ship, *Minghe Hao*, all the way to Jamaica.

Made in China come every day and every day I tell him

101

another piece of myself. He eat up my words like food on a plate. I marry to a man twenty years older than me; he old and sick and not much help, so I give Made in China a job sweeping up shop and washing down the counters. Sometimes after I finish with my story, Made in China tell me his. His words choke in his throat and hard to come out and one day I stretch him on the bed and lie down next to him and he cry in my hair. We stay like that for a long time and I open my blouse and he suckle my breast.

Made in China, I say, when I come to Jamaica I have a baby boy in my belly. On the ship I only eat rice and when I arrive I so small, only seventy-five pounds. Baby boy die one week after, they take him from me and bury him in a grave mark with two milk tins. After that, they don't know what to do with me, then someone from the ship find Mr. Ying shop and give me to him and he marry me.

Every day Made in China suckle at my breasts. He don't do nothing else. He just suckle. Made in China, I say, your hair smell like pimento and pimento remind me of something in China but I can't remember what. I not Chinese anymore, you know. I am Jamaica Chinie and when you are Chinie you allowed to forget. In China my name was Shuzhen but here they call me Susan. I like Susan better.

One day Made in China folding boxes when he suddenly stop and say, "You poison your husband." "Bull shit," I say. I learn to say bull shit from watching movie, when I say those words I stand tough and set my mouth like salt june plum, but it do nothing to this boy. He suckle my breast every day and he know all my softness. I close the shop and take him in the back and tell him my business.

Made in China, I say, a long time ago I give a man poison in his bath water. The poison travel in his pores and bloat him up and turn him purple. He look like eggplant.

For one month Made in China disappear. I think I lose him. Mr. Ying getting weaker and weaker and I need help in the shop. Made in China the only person I trust. On the day he come back I make him chicken foot soup and I tell him the rest.

Made in China, I say, listen to this fairy tale with no laughing ending. A long time ago I used to be beautiful; there was no marks on my skin and my eyebrows curve around like two arches to paradise. I work in a shop massaging feet and filing rich people toe nails. One day, as I rub a man's soft heels, he asked me to marry him. He have sixteen fishing boats and a house with tiger lilies in front and fans hanging from the ceiling inside. I see how he ugly, but I say yes because he promise to bring my little sister over from Vietnam. I live with this man seven years and every year, I beg him to bring her over and every year he promise me yes, but never do it. I see that he have no intention and because of how he lie every little thing about him make me hate him more – his toes shrivel like figs in his sandals, his sweaty palms on my flesh, the rankness of his breath. Eight years I live with him and one day I get letter that my sister dead from dengue fever and that is the day I decide to kill him. Made in China, I say, don't tell a word.

One day me and Made in China lay down on the sofa. He had his head in my shirt and Mr. Ying was upstairs. Mr. Ying too weak to come down by himself so I wasn't worried about that. I love Mr. Ying and would never hurt him. In my dealings with him, I make up for every bad thing in my past; I make him three meals a day; I keep the house clean; I run the shop when he's sick; read to him; shave him; bath him and give him enema and wash him down with bay rum; not even mosquito dare bite him if I can help it. But from the start Mr. Ying too old and I try to keep my feelings secret but every now and then I need someone touch me.

Mr. Ying wet the bed and must be was calling me, but I never hear him, his voice so weak. Then I surprise he do it, but he raise himself off the bed and hold on to the wall and make his way out the room. I hear a voice behind me, Shuzhen, and when I turn around he standing there at the top of the stairs looking down on me and on Made in China. I so shame, me all exposed, Made in China with his mouth at my breast.

Everything downhill after that. I so shame. I can't go back to China; I can't stay here. All night Mr. Ying up there rotting in the stink sheets, won't let me wash him. I bring him soup and he won't drink it, he think I go poison him. Made in China disappear again, this time for good. My one baby bury in the cemetery, starve to death, the poor little thing. I so tired, I just want to die.

In the before day, the sky barely yellow, I leave Mr. Ying sleeping and go out in the yard. I take a piece of rope from the side of the house, tie it to the tamarind tree and loop it around my neck. Something catch up in my throat, my feet dance a little dance, and then I feel my breath leave, settling in the branches; and the breath want to fill something and it find a swarm of flies and the flies swirl around, all crazy with my shit.

Later when the crowd gather, the girl, Dahlia, crane her neck to see me. A woman break out praying, speaking in tongues. Mr. Ying, watching through the window, a fly on his eyelid. No worry, someone will take care of him – his sister in St. Catherine, the Chins from across the way. But look Dahlia still craning her neck to see me in my nightie, my breasts hanging down, my legs swaying slight in the breeze.

Too late, little Dahlia, too late. Made in China done suck him milk and gone.

Mrs. Ying's voice came to me suddenly; running like eye-water down the page right after I fed her doll pomegranate and green mango soaked in salt. Her tears stained the tablecloth, but unlike Alva's, they had no distinct smell. Coopie was sleeping in front of the T.V. and Girl was in bed sucking her thumb. I got up and closed the kitchen door and began to sweep, my pen stuck behind my ear. Sister decided to absent herself, though only the day before she taunted me out in the yard, "Mind what you write."

"Is you put me up to this!" I shouted, and she cut her eye and walked away. She came back later in the afternoon, smoking a spliff and blowing rings through her nose. I saw her pass by the gate but she kept on walking and did not stop.

I picture Mrs. Ying bright as pink coral vine, hanging in her nightgown. At first I am disappointed in her. I had wanted her to be strong and lion-heart like that woman she had been who crossed seas in the bottom of a cargo ship. But tonight, after sweeping the kitchen three times, I accept Mrs. Ying for who she is. She sits now on the windowsill hoping this story will make her clean.

Sister Carmen, too, waits in the wings. All these years she has kept Willa's bangles, too fearful to deliver them, not enough blood in the communion cup to cover her transgression. Meanwhile, Alva is fat; her sister's story ready to break inside of her. She craves more and more to eat, and I spend all my savings trying to feed her. If I am not careful, she will even steal food from Girl's mouth. At night, Dahlia and Made in China tap impatiently on the kitchen table while I am sleeping. Only when I get up and turn on the light do they stop. I am just an ordinary woman with a handful of words, but each doll presses, waiting for me to tell all.

F.T.

Alva's Spoken Word Story #4

"Stop crying or go home," the supervisor come to me and say. The woman beside me make like she don't hear. She keep her head straight, sewing her quick neat seams. The more you sew, the more you earn – but not much – 3 cents for each garment. She dreams of her children and their curly eyelash daddy left behind in Haiti. I wipe the tears from my eyes, adjust the mask they give to protect from dust. The supervisor watches from across the room and I set my face like a flint; I must keep my tears on the inside; I will not let him win.

As my needle comes undone, I hold the thread, picturing it long like the red string unraveling from the woman's headscarf in my dream. Tonight, I mean to follow her.

At six o'clock, I pick up my paycheck, spit on the ground in front of the manager's office, and leave. All the way on the A train, eye-water coming down my face, smell just like the medicine Mama used to wash me down with as a child. I so hungry and the hungry can't stop; something inside all troubled and feverish.

<u>Willa's Background Vocals (Bob on the Juke Box)</u>

This could be the first trumpet/

(As recorded from Carmen Innocencia's window)

PART FOUR

THE NARROW GATE

The time which followed Mrs. Ying's death was what Madda Shilling called the season of the bougainvillea, the blossoms blooming pink and orange and purple in every corner of the yard. At certain times of day, little whirlwinds caught up the petals, blowing them everywhere, Dahlia and Madda Shilling going outside and standing in the midst of it, their arms outstretched.

Madda Shilling's yard could almost be missed from outside the street – the bougainvillea fence growing high and unruly, the gate partly covered with oleander. Still, every now and then someone came calling to buy a dose of Madda's roots, for always there were bottles of various sizes displayed on a table on the verandah, the labels with names like chaney root, raw moon, leaf-of-life, sinkle bible, ram goat roses, god-bush, search-mi-heart. *This one will cure block up sinus; that one will give yu strong heart; take this if yu have sex problem; and see that one in the tall bottle? Drink it only if yu want pregnant and mix it good with red beet, especially if yu want the baby to healthy. That one in the soda bottle will clear up morning sickness, but if the baby father ugly, don't bother ask me to make him pickney pretty.*

The customers left with their precious bottle of something huddled under their arm; Madda Shilling calling, "Walk good, yu hear?" their backs disappearing through the narrow gate. After school, Dahlia helped Madda search for bush to make her tonics. She sketched in her exercise book, writing the bush names in ink while Madda dried leaves on the back porch or soaked roots in a pan, wind puffing at her white hair.

It was two weeks before Christmas and Alva sent Dahlia a snow dome; inside there was a girl and two pine trees and a dog with a green vest. When Dahlia shook it, snow filled the glass, the girl's face full of light and Dahlia wanted to be that girl, so safe there in her dome, her hands in wool mittens, the earth revolving on its axis only for her. She shook the dome over and over, not wanting the snow to stop, the girl ever joyful, the little dog's ears pricked up. Each time the air filled with bougainvillea in Madda Shilling's yard, Dahlia became that girl – if only for a moment before she remembered the guinep seed in her throat ready to burst again.

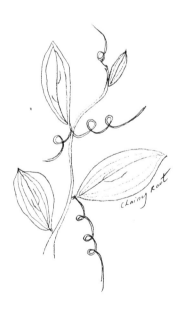

Chainy Root

Dahlia's Bougainvillea Chorus

Soon as school done, I run to Madda's yard and start draw the bougainvillea. I draw every vein, every pollen. I make names for the flowers-them – "Mary Sunday Baggy," "Mary Monday Baggy," and on like that. I make sure Mary have a baggy to wear every day of the week. I find a leaf with blight on it, and called it "Mary Dutty Baggy." I draw another one with blossoms blowing every which way out the window and called it, "Mary Can't Mek up her Mind Which Baggy to Wear." Drawing the pictures make Madda Shilling laugh, and the guinep in my throat grow little smaller.

Sometimes I draw Alva putting on lipstick under the mango tree or Mama threading her needle on Madda Shilling's verandah, Daddy holding up a rum bottle of honey to the sun. In all the picture-them, Madda Shilling watching from the window, or the side of the house, or the chicken coop; Made in China making a monkey face and me making one back, and always bougainvillea falling everywhere, filling all the white space.

The bougainvillea make me dream long dreams and in one of the dreams-them I see an orange snail on a rock. I try my best not to let it out my sight, but I stop to tie my shoe-lace and the snail disappear. All evening I search for the snail until the sun set pink like Mrs. Ying's nightie. Madda Shilling call me inside to eat, my plate fix with liver in brown gravy, two boiled dumplings, a piece of dasheen and a slice of tomato. We drink sugar-water squeeze with lime and Madda Shilling say, "Is full moon tonight, time to plant gungu."

113

Later when I sure she sleeping, I go outside in my barefoot, the yard light up pretty-pretty with stars. On the front steps I see what look like piece of silver ribbon, but when I look good again, I see that is the snail's trail. The trail all glitter-up and I touch it with my finger and find it can read just like braille: *Is late and I'm up sweeping the kitchen. All day, story been on my mind. Just as I am about to lean the broom against the back door...* I rub my fingers across the concrete, so hungry and craven for the snail's voice, so sorry it did rain after dinner, washing so much away.

When I wake up, bougainvillea petals on my pillow. I push them into my plaits like Alva hiding money in her hair. Whole day I wonder about snail woman sweeping her kitchen and the something that happened just as she was about to lean her broom against the door. When Madda Shilling call for me to brush up the yard, I do not complain. I say, "Coming Madda," sweeping every corner, hoping to find the missing bits of story. I wish I coulda find one more line, one more shine word. Just as I turn over a mango leaf, I see it – the snail's trail, all silver and bright. I rub my finger over it same like in the dream, Madda Shilling watching from the side of the house.

December 12, 2002

Two weeks till the 24th and Christmas Card Girl's expected appearance. When she appears I will be right at
the curbside, waiting with the silver bangles Sister Carmen sent. The bangles are curled at the ends like a
lizard's tail and Carmen shined them up nice with coconut
oil and a soft cloth.

It's true, I remember Willa from Mrs. Murdock's grade
three. We used to play jacks out in the school yard. She
liked the metal kind because of the sound they made
when they fell on the ground; and she won every time,
scooping everything in her small, quick hands. Afterwards, she would disappear down a little lane behind the
corner shop, her dolly wrapped in a blanket in her
schoolbag.

I remember the day I followed her home, tracing her
steps through dust. Her mother was outside washing
clothes and the yard was filled with pea doves. Every now
and then one of the pea doves flew onto the brim of the
wash basin and Mona shooed it away with a click-click of
her tongue. Willa helped wring clothes and hang them on
the line and when they were done mother and daughter
sat on the steps and ate bulla cake and butter, the doves
congregating around them, nesting in Mona's lap, in
Willa's thick hair. I was only ten years old, but remember
the distinct feeling they had a language all their own –
the birds calling, Willa and Mona answering back.

Today I bought a set of metal jacks for the Willa doll, same as the ones we used to play with. She has started to steal now, just like Cedar Mary - first my earrings, the paper clip on my notebook, the spoons on the dish rack. Between Alva's eating and Willa's stealing, I have time for nothing else; every half hour a little something falling, ting!, a reminder to refill Alva's saucer, her bowl with coconut milk. Meanwhile, Willa continues to hum - she likes to do background for Marley and sometimes Lovindeer, but what she wants most is to just let loose and reel out her own tune.

I put my pen behind my ear and go feed the pea doves a piece of stale bread. Girl runs out behind me.

"Is who Miss Mary, Mama?"

Willa's Background Hum

Listen careful, you will hear/

(As recorded from Carmen Innocencia's window)

<u>Letters from Sister Carmen Innocencia:</u>

December 16, 2002

Today I took communion and the wine taste all weak like it water-down.

December 17, 2002

The truth is, not even the Pope-self would believe what going on.

December 18, 2002

Nightfall and the poinsettias outside my window getting redder and redder.

December 19, 2002

All Mother Angelica have to do is ring the chapel bell, ting!, and my heart jump.

All day the Made in China doll looks through the window. I feed him coconut drops just like the ones in Mrs. Ying's showcase.

Coopie is in the kitchen making Christmas pudding. The aroma of red wine, vanilla and brown sugar fills the house, mingling with the smell of Alva's tears. Girl is licking the mixing bowl with her tongue; there are Mary's boy-child carols on the radio. The house feels electric, the Christmas Card Madonna making her way toward Papine.

F.T.

Kingston breeze flutters the pages of your notebook, and what are you afraid of? Of harming Girl? Of losing Coopie? Of becoming the story? Alva's shoes fit so well, but she already has a twin. Who are you?

11

Each day Madda Shilling's bougainvillea bloomed more and more beautiful, people stopping to peer in the yard, asking the price for a bottle of something on the ledge, begging a cutting of croton, poking their finger into an angel's trumpet. It was on one of those afternoons, magenta petals falling all around, that a young man appeared at Madda's gate. His hair was pushed into a yellow tam and he had a light beard, a satchel over his shoulder. As Dahlia walked towards him, she saw his eyes shiny-shiny and bright. He put his hands to his mouth and pulled his lips apart, crossed his eyes into a monkey face.

Humming Fish

Made in China's Version

Mrs. Ying smell like curry and scotch pepper. She take me in the back and nurse me and is like the room just swaying, the two of us crossing sea in the bottom of a big ship. All afternoon rain falling, and the water rise up higher and higher till it catch the window. Mrs. Ying don't pay it no mind, she rock me and sing-song me, and next time I look, water cover up the whole glass, cray fish and coral weed floating by. Me and Mrs. Ying travel the Seven Seas, the room full up with bags of rice and flour and crates of ginger ale and cooking oil.

"I remember your mother," Mrs. Ying say. "When her belly was big I used to watch her in the street with her beautiful goose walk."

I close my eyes and listen the rain, another fish swim pass and stare through the window. It open and shut its mouth like it want speak.

"No mind, Made in China," Mrs. Ying say. "Every year now Milly fly south with all the other mothers, come to find their left-behind children."

Someone's shoe float by in the water and I say to Mrs. Ying, "That one look like yours," but she don't hear me. She still thinking on Mama's wings spread wide in flight.

"Watch careful; she will come when you least suspect."

When Mrs. Ying dead, I go to the funeral and I watch them put her inna the ground. Nobody never see me because I stand off in the bush to the side and wear a dark shades. Mr. Ying was there in a wheelchair with few of his cousins and a woman playing guitar. All of Mr. Ying family bury in Dove Cot but no Dove Cot money spend on Mrs. Ying; she bury right with the love bush and soda bottles and the mad people-them.

Whole heap o coral vine was all around and is right there at Mrs. Ying graveside it come to me to bring back Daddy honey. Money tight but I start up a little thing in the market. People love my honey and when they ask me where it come from, I don't say a word. I keep few hives in different abandon property across town and one special one in the cemetery. That honey is a special honey and when people eat it is like they can't get enough. One woman come to me and say, after she bathe at night, she rub it on her skin and if you ever see how her husband turn sweet on her; another one tell me say she mix it with Guinness and a raw egg and drink it down and when she done, she bruck cane with her bare hands.

I mix little of the honey with irish moss myself, and I smoke two spliff under the poui tree, and I don't know if is the honey or the spliff but I dream see Alva, she same one, cover up in bees and waving from the back of a bus.

I so happy to dream see Alva that same as I wake up, I run out in the street. A bus was at the corner and before I coulda even think, a woman in a red head-tie, stretch her neck out the window and say "Step right in!" I get on the bus and ride it all the way to Portland.

When I reach, bougainvillea everywhere and the sea so pretty I spend a whole week just watching the ships-them and eating bread and drop-down mango. The beach

full up with gulls and I wonder to myself, "Is which one
is Mama?" All week I smoke my spliff and talk to the
birds, "The honey sweet, but night-time I still cry." One
evening because my money done and because I need a
fare to get back to town, I pick up a stone and knock on
a gate by the road; I see a girl on the verandah combing
out dandelion from an old lady hair.

A dandelion chute from Madda Shilling's garden lands on my notebook. The dandelions in Madda's yard are three feet tall and too beautiful to weed. She picks the leaves, tossing them with clover and ram-goat-roses.

I am writing in the kitchen again. Girl has been sleeping for a whole hour, her breathing soft, a little lizard exposing its red and yellow tongue on the floor beside her. Coopie is sitting on the back steps polishing his shoes. I just saw Willa steal change from his pocket, the coins clinking on red tile. Coopie looks around, uneasy. His eyes catch mine and I smile mischievously, turn up the radio and drop another cornmeal dumpling in the boiling pot.

Today is winter solstice, Alva's birthday. I make her a bowl of rice seasoned with salt-fish, wrap her head with a fresh cloth, make a new patch for her eye.

The streets in town are full of madness. So much traffic and noise force-ripes the mangoes, makes the coconuts drop before their time. Sister has left a present on the windowsill. It is wrapped in banana leaf and tied with a piece of string. I dare not open it.

F.T.

The temptation to search for Cedar Mary has got the better of me. Much as I don't like it, I leave Girl with Coopie's mother and head to the cemetery in search of the Madonna. I have chosen Sunday because on weekends there are always funerals in progress and this deters some of the troublemakers. This time the caretaker is not there and the grounds are even more overgrown than before. The tombstones are littered with soda cans and beer bottles; a man is asleep under a piece of cardboard. I make my way carefully over love bush and macca, looking for Dahlia's poui tree, my only marker. Without its yellow September flowers, I am unable to find it.

By the time I find my way back to the entrance, the last of the funerals has started to break up. The mourners leave with careful, quick steps and without looking back.

Back on the street, Sister repeats her old advice, this time on a piece of paper slipped behind the windshield wiper of my car: *mind what story you tell*. A beef patty and a bottle of coconut water are left for me on the seat. There are two days remaining until Christmas Card Girl's return.

F.T.

Alva's Spoken Word Story #6

treasures/ one-eye/ cheekbones/ job/ walk/
calling/ angle/ way/ home/ clothing/ slim/ set/ uptown/
China/ hair/ through/ half/ red/ bus/ walk/ tree/
street/ drivers/ out/ sun/ Dahlia/ catch/ top

Milly and Clive never raise me to go to America and
sew rich people draws. I woulda prefer dead than stay
here one more day. The woman with the pen behind her
ear come to me in my dream. She feed me patty and
coconut water and wipe the tears from my eye. I take
all the words out my pocket and hold them out to her.
She look at them all bright and silver in the moonlight
and she take them and arrange them and string them
one-one on a piece of thread and tie them just like shine
charms around my waist.

As she turn to leave, I grab after the red scarf
trailing behind, and this time I catch it and she turn
around and say, "Come, let me show you your true face."

gungu/pepper/patty/move/rundown/guava/soursop/
swim/book/hog/shoot/thread/

Alva's decision to return to Jamaica surprises me. Her doll has grown taller, head and shoulders above the others; her hand rests on her hip, her lip set with determination.

Sister appears at the back door. She is six years old and has two plaits and missing front teeth.

"Characters have a way of taking over," she says.

I glance at her then keep on writing.

"Give Alva your pen so she can find her way back home."

Sister takes the lollipop from her mouth and offers me a lick. It tastes like brown sugar and pineapple. I give it back to her and she skips into the yard and disappears.

Much as I care about Alva, I cannot leave her with my pen. What if she frightens Girl or steals my skin? I want out of this story. I want to find the way to the back gate.

Sister's head appears at the window. Her plaits stick out from the side of her face and she grins, the lollipop still in her mouth.

"One writer gave up both her lungs," she says.

"Enough," I say, "leave me alone."

She sticks out her tongue. "Another one got stuck in story and never came out."

In an old shoe box I find a photo of me shelling peas on the verandah. I am smiling, both eyes big and bright. I cut around an eye and glue my seeing one over Alva's dreaming one. Pain darts through my left socket and I bite on a kitchen towel trying to hold back the scream in my throat. All night I toss in bed, my eye throbbing and full of Alva's dreams. Coopie reaches out for me in his sleep, "Alva," he calls me, "Alva."

Next morning, I lay my pen at Alva's feet. For the first time in months, I do not smell her tears.

F.T.

III

In the slanted light of the doorway, Madda watched Dahlia and Made in China at the gate, the wind puffing her round white hair, sending little parachutes across the yard. That evening she gave Made in China fried sprats and bread and opened the windows in the room prepared with a cot and a small table, a hibiscus in a jar. The streets had changed him; he was quiet and contemplative; he had a missing finger and there was a scar over his left eye which Dahlia did not remember. Over dinner he and Dahlia glanced at each other shyly, exchanging smiles and Madda put more fish on his plate. Later, because she did not know where to begin, Dahlia said, "I saw Mrs. Ying hanging from the tamarind tree."

Made in China slept late the next morning, the scent of rose water on the pillows, luring him deeper into dream. In the afternoon he and Dahlia worked in the garden, raking the mango leaves, trimming the hibiscus hedge, planting pepper seeds for Madda's cure for sex problem.

"Is what her milk did taste like?"

"Thick and sweet."

"But why you drink it?"

"She take me for her son."

"If Mama could hear you now."

Work into the night mi love –
letters small and tight –
until the moon, eating her own flesh,
disappears.

The time has come to pay respect to the muse for it is she who has guided you here thus far. Honor the history of your craft and make her doll with special care, tracing her back one chosen word at a time.

Invitation

First you start with her belly – a large mango seed that you wash with rainwater, then leave on the zinc roof to dry in the sun. After three days, lean your ladder against the wall and climb back up to take a look. The seed will be shrunken and bleached white. Hold it carefully in your palm; feel it warm as a fresh egg.

Use your penknife to make a thin slit through the seed's side; then soak it overnight in a half cup of white rum. Next morning, check on it again before leaving it to dry on the roof once more. After four days, you will see that the slit has widened, the inside a faint yellow.

Sit at the kitchen table and stuff the belly well with ground pimento, thyme, salt, pepper, and a little rosemary; then write the word "speak" on a piece of dried banana leaf, folding it tight and sliding it inside. Tie the stuffed belly with a strip of muslin, winding it securely.

The head is to be made from an almond seed. After it is washed and sun-dried, write her name – Sister, Sister, Sister – around and around in tiny letters, then wear it tied tight right over your navel. After seven days, take it off and attach it to the mango belly.

The arms and legs are next – twigs broken from a tamarind switch. Spanish moss will do for her hair and two seashells for her breasts. A bag of glass beads makes perfect embellishment. Attach them one by one – red and green and blue; then adorn with gold thread as you see fit. Paint a generous mouth and two eyes wide open; a single cowrie should hang from her hair.

Pouring Libation

Feed Sister yellow cornmeal and white rum. Place fresh bougainvillea at her feet along with a bowl of uncooked rice filled with coins. When you are ready, tie a red ribbon around a ballpoint pen. Put it in your bag along with a loaf of bread, a bottle of soda, a packet of pow-dered milk, a kerosene lamp, two red candles, and a small hand mirror. Go outside and keep on walking until you come to a place where the road splits like your legs pushing out a child. Choose the path with the most gravel. To the left there will be a julie mango tree with a snake carved into its bark. When you see this, switch your bag to the other shoulder and keep on going. You will need to hurry if you are to make it to the river before sundown. The last thing you need is for your shadow to beat you there, snatching away the words waiting at the water bottom.

As soon as you arrive, take the bread from the bag; break it into small pieces and cast it in an arc upon the water. Open the bottle of soda and pour it slowly; sprin-kle the milk powder and watch it disappear downstream. This is the time to light the red candles and the kerosene lamp. When at last you reach for the pen, the ink will ooze like shed blood. Do not lift your hand from the page. Do not stop to scratch your scalp, slap the mosquito at your ankle, or brush the fly from your chin. Most of all, do not worry about the crocodile eyeing from the other side of the river. Cut your eye, spit over your shoulder, and keep on writing. You must write until there is no more ink left in your pen.

Signs and Wonders

Later, when the moon appears, the dogs upstream will begin barking. You will know when Sister is ready, her chest softly rattling – took-took, took-took – like so many seeds. From the corner of your eye, catch a glimpse of her sitting on a warm rock to the side, her face in her palm. Know that she has traveled from a long way – two hundred years through cane fields, swamp, grass-lice, wind, rain, and mango blossom. See how twigs fall from the nutmeg tree each time she blinks to adjust her eyes to river light.

She has come to observe your hand busy as a small bird, reminding her of a night long ago, when she leaned against a moonshine windowsill, scratching on wood and dry leaf with a pen stolen from Massa and marked with his initials. How she hungered for words then, devouring them wherever they could be found – the bottoms of cracked plates, the inside soles of shoes, the rims of old biscuit tins. She worked into the night, tiny letters like soldier ants, racing across bark.

A quick glance at Sister, and see how she cranes her neck, closes her eyes, listening to the rhythm of your pen. Someone is probably throwing stones into the river, trying to distract you, but do not look up or you will break the spell, ink turning to scab before it reaches the page. Concentrate instead on the two flickering candles with long red tears, for it is your busy hand that keeps Sister breathing, and whatever you do, you must not lose her. Write write write her name over and over, bringing her back to the next morning, her fingers stained night blue and hidden in shallow pockets against her thighs. When Mistress called, she quickly took the egg basket and scurried away so she could wash with water from the chicken trough. She washed and washed, but the blue remained. Two brown eggs fell onto the floor. A door banged shut; footsteps approached from across the yard.

As you write the word, "yard", fireflies circle the kerosene lamp, and you notice a man's foot on the rock beside you. Resist the temptation to run away. There is no escape now; Sister has taken you all the way back – two hundred years through the smell of molasses. Hold your head still as the man sharpens his machete. Pretend to be interested in crushed corn on the ground. Leaves rustle underfoot, and you hear Sister scream, her voice high-pitched and broken in the evening sky.

This is the scene in which blood trickles everywhere, words lodged in your throat like fresh bone. As Sister's amputated fingers are hurled through the air, stuff your scarf in your mouth to stop your lips from trembling. Grab the fingers quick before the dogs arrive. Bloody nails dig into your skin now, and you want out of this story, as far away as you can possibly hide. You almost dash your pen to the ground, but then for one brief moment, Sister's eyes meet yours.

Remember a woman who got stuck in story, wandered around and around and never came back? They found her shoes by the edge of the river with a note inside which read, *The word made flesh*... Better to have stayed at home – hung the clothes on the line, stirred the cornmeal porridge, swept under the bed. But you cannot change your mind anymore; you are too far gone. A small crow cries in the lime tree behind you.

Closing the Space

This is the time for the hand-mirror in your shoulder bag.
Reach for it with your left hand and lean it against the
rock in front of you. The mirror sees trouble before you
do and will always remember the way back home. Sister
still screams a trail of red, and you must hurry before she
disappears. Chase the trail all the way through the bush;
howl if you must, your voice joining hers; follow the
course of the river as she runs downstream.

You will see Sister pause at the river's mouth; note
how she beckons you with her bottomless eyes. Late as it
is, the moon has almost eaten all its flesh; the crocodile
sleeps at the water's edge. In the square of the hand-
mirror, glance back down the path from which you came.
Way at the end of it, you will see your little yellow
kitchen, the table set with clear glass plates. A lizard
stretches on a straw mat by the stove. Sugar ants cluster
around crumbs on the windowsill. As Massa's hungry dogs
race toward Sister, spell out her name; press into the
page as you urge her on, your pen almost empty.

You have heard stories of slaves in flight, flying back to
Africa, but this is not that story. You have heard stories of
women walking out into the ocean, drowning themselves,
but this is not that story.

In this story, you must follow Sister's heels until the
river falls into the waiting sea. In wee morning light, the
Caribbean is thick as dark ink. You wade into the water,
and it licks your flesh with a warm blue tongue. Massa's
three dogs arrive only inches behind you, hesitating at the
water's edge. Sister turns around and grabs at your collar,
pulls you down flat against the ocean floor. You hold on
to each other, plaits afloat in blue fluid. When you open
your eyes, you see the dog's paws paddling above. Your
lungs are swollen, and you cannot hold your breath much

longer, soon you must rise up for air. You turn to look at Sister and notice her face: The sockets of her eyes are generations deep; the pupils like searchlights burrow into yours. As your head fills with yellow light, you recognize each other as next of kin. She pulls a string from her navel – two hundred years long – coils it into a ball, presses it in your hand. You want to reach her, to make some gesture –

But you are out of air. Somewhere a whip cracks, and you rise from the water, arms extended. As your blood pumps faster, the dogs hurl themselves at Sister's flesh. Do not try to save her – there is no more time and not enough ink for indecision. Keep one eye on the mirror and turn now, go. Run back down the gravel path, past the julie mango tree and back to the place where the road splits like your legs throwing away a child. Dry your tears on your sleeve and keep on going. Do not look back; this scene cannot be revised.

As you enter the yard, the little ball unravels behind you, expanding in the wind like a long red cloth. Fold it carefully before you enter the house; then write your name in the middle of your hand. Trace the lines of your palm, crisscrossed and dusty. Call yourself out loud – hear how your voice has changed.

* * *

December 23, 2002

Sister waits for me on a rock in the yard. She is in her prime, long-legged and strong. When I look closer, I see the dog's teeth marks on her arms and neck.

"Why you didn't tell me before?" I ask, and for the first time I can remember, her eyes flood and she looks away.

F.T.

134

Coopie's cakes are all ready and I have made red sorrel
drink flavored with ginger. Me and Girl have decorated
the house with paper garlands and by tomorrow the place
will be busy with cousins and neighbors from the yard
next door.

In spite of all the craziness, I return to the cemetery
once again. This time I take the Dahlia doll with me. It is
noon, and there is a funeral in progress for the deceased
girlfriend of a government official. People say she ended
up dead because she knew too much politics (but that's
another story). Once again, I cannot find the poui tree.

I leave by the east gate and just as I am about to turn
away, I notice a woman standing there. She is wearing a
yellow dress and my old sandals. It is Alva, dark woman of
the high cheekbones. She has a shopping bag held close to
her side and she appears not to notice me. I watch her
run to catch a bus and I quickly follow it all the way to
Papine where she exits and stands by the side of the road,
across from a betting shop piazza. A small crowd has
gathered to see Christmas Card Girl who has appeared as
expected at the appointed time. Her hum rises up as she
closes her eyes and rocks the baby Jesus back and forth.
A woman drops money in the diaper bag at her feet and
Christmas Card Girl just keeps on humming.

A truck rushes by blowing leaves and trash in its path.
Across the street, Alva steadies herself on the curb. Her
eye patch is made of black felt and in its center she has
sewn a pair of full orange lips, the word, "now", embroi-
dered underneath. I am standing at the edge of the
crowd. I take the bangles from my pocket and drop them
in the diaper bag. Falling among coins at the bottom, the
bangles chime, the sound traveling as if from afar,
through the eyes of hurricanes, the riff of a Marley tune,

the open mouth of a woman in labor, dropping ting-ting in a swirl of dust and nutmeg. For the first time, Christmas Card Girl stops humming and opens her eyes. She reaches for the bangles and holds them like silver butterflies in her palm. "Willa," I say and she looks up at me and smiles, the same smile of years ago, both of us ten years old, a baby doll in her school bag, her fist full of jacks.

I put the bangles on her wrist and she places the baby Jesus in my arms. He smells of flour and baby oil. His little feet kick against my belly-bottom and he whispers, "So, you are here," before he closes his eyes and turns again to rubber. When I look up, Willa is already pushing her way through the crowd and walking down the street. Half of the crowd remains watching me with the baby Jesus and the other half follows Christmas Card Girl toward the market. Carmen Innocencia watches from a window above the bar; I pay no attention. The baby wakes up and, instinctively, I hold him against my chest and rub his back; he sighs and burps. I turn to look into his eyes, but they are closed again, polyurethane rubber.

"Willa!" I call, but she keeps on walking, straight toward Alva. They glance at each other – for only a moment – Alva with her one eye, Willa still smiling, her mouth full of silver teeth. The bangles jingle and Christmas breeze flirts at Alva's skirt as she steps off the curb, turning ever so briefly to watch the shiny-teeth woman already disappearing down the road. Her feet hurt and she sits on the steps of the betting shop piazza, takes off her shoes; Willa walking away toward the smell of fresh fish, pimento and thyme, a small following still close behind. Small birds lined up on a cable wire mark the edge of the world and down in the betting shop some-one's horse leaps across the finish line. I rock the baby Jesus in my arms and cry.

Room above a Bar in Papine: Carmen's Praise-song

My prayer necklace burst and all the john crow beads-
them scatter out the window, Mary Mother-of-All,
switching her hips down the street, her dreads trailing
behind, the bangles ting-ting so sweet on her wrist,
hallelujah. What a blessedness, what a joy divine, the
baby Jesus in Flamingo's arms.

IV

Alva and Dahlia and Made in China spent Christmas in Portland. They ate black cake on a quiet stretch of beach and threw stones into the water. It was Alva who threw the most, tracing the three of them across sea and limestone and gully and bird feather, back to the house with the zinc roof. They stayed there on the beach until night, walking along the shore, little stars sequined against the sky. Madda had given them a bag of candles which they stopped to light and stick in the sand. Music played in a bar out on the road and they were all giddy from the bottle of rum passed between them, the horizon tilted ever so slightly, Dahlia giggling and filling her bra with shells.

All week Made in China had been keeping a secret and only when they had drunk the last of the rum and it was almost time to go, did he open his satchel and take her out – Cedar Mary, a little smile on her face. Dahlia giggled and put her hand over her mouth and the Christmas lights on Alva's eye-patch blinked on and off.

So, the big moment has come and gone. Willa and Alva should have recognized each other, kissed and embraced in the middle of the street? At the edge of the world, the roofs tilt lop-side and fiction is strange and truth stranger and knives and forks do not always match.

Sister Story-ma waits for me under the ackee tree; she has returned to her favorite guise, an old woman.

"Your pen finish," I say, handing it back to her, and she smiles and shows her mossy teeth.

"Everything done now and I want back my life; I want Coopie and Girl and curry and rice and -"

"Not so easy," she says, flipping through pages, "Mary boy-chile sleeping, but what if I wake him up?" She reaches deep down inside her brassiere, pulls out a pen twice as long as the first.

I take it from her; kiss my teeth and go inside, locking the back door and pushing a chair behind it.

Somewhere in a Kingston yard, Willa belts out a tune and God's little shine things fall from the sky.

F.T.
Kingston, Jamaica

AFTER WORD

This story moves in circles. It flies like a bird around the roof of your house, twittering its evening song, its wings fluttering soft like the nylon curtains left to dry on the clothes line.

You sit eating your dinner of steamed calalloo, salt-fish and fried dumplings. You drink your tea sweetened with one teaspoon brown sugar, one teaspoon condensed milk; you set the spoon on the table and have the half-conscious feeling that something is afoot. Maybe it's the sudden calm in the sea-sick coconut leaves, the pause in the line of sugar ants on the floor, the hush of your child's breathing. Tea rolling down the side of the cup, you wait for the brown liquid to meet the calico table cloth.

Out in the yard, a neighbor calls for you and in that moment, the feeling quickly passes.

As you open the front door, you do not notice the bird flying off into the distance, her beak clutching guinea grass plucked from your garden, the broken end of a story trailing behind her.

APPENDIX

A. <u>Dreams</u>

Around the middle of the story, I began recording my dreams:

1. I am driving along a country road at night and spot a man in the middle of a field. He is holding a flashlight and shining it on the ground. Words sprout up and down each row everywhere the light touches.

2. A sepia photo – a young woman dressed as in the 1920's, her hands clasped in front of her, a silk zig-zag patterned scarf around her neck. I call her Z.

3. Birds everywhere.

4. Z. appears again. She throws her scarf over her shoulder. This time I know who she is.

5. Slugs everywhere. Fat and brown and always going places. I heap them on a plate and sprinkle them with salt. I am eating my ancestors.

6. My daughter calling out to me.

7. A dictionary full of definitions of the same word...

8. Blue thread

9. Red thread

10. Thread

11. I have heard of writers who live in far off places where the snow comes down all soft like flour falling through a sieve. In such countries, the temperature can drop low enough to freeze ink in a pen. I had a dream once that I lived in such a place. In this dream, I was bundled in a sweater, crossing a busy intersection and thinking about Alva. In the distance, there were moun-

tains – bare and flat – but what I remember most about that dream was the absence of birds. I reached into my pocket to find my pen for I wanted so much to remember this curiosity, but then the light flashed green and I had to move on.

I awoke to find myself sitting on my verandah with the taste of ripe blueberries in my mouth (or at least what I thought was the taste of blueberries.) I immediately walked out into the yard, my bare feet in the warm dust. So familiar it was to live here in this little pale blue house with five square windows, a zinc roof for making music when it rains and neighbors cussing across the fence. I reached into my pocket to find my pen, for I wanted so much to remember this day, this first of October.

12. October 7, 2002. Maybe it was the ripe banana I ate before going to bed, but last night there I was again at the same busy intersection, my collar pulled up against the wind. Even as I stood there, waiting for the light to change, I was conscious of the pillow on which my head lay, printed with faint bamboo outlines. This time I knew that the birds flown south were the same ones nesting in the lime tree outside my window. And there on the curb, snow blowing at my feet, I felt something new – a stone lodged in my throat. I awoke; the light changing green, my foot in midair.

All night I lay in bed wondering at the weight of a stone.

B. Of Boats and Dandelions and the Swirling of Thoughts

1. In the margin of my page, I am drawing pictures of boats. Madda Shilling's father was buried in a fishing boat; the boat's name was *Baby She*, named after a girl from his youth. His relatives made a lid for Baby She and lowered it into the red dirt behind his mother's house, just as the grandfather had requested.

I think to myself that the bottom of a boat must be a good place to rest. I draw a picture of Baby She, filling it with dandelions and I imagine the father sitting in the flower filled boat and sailing out to sea, leaving Jamaica and the girl he loved behind.

My daughter yawns and I turn the page; I picture the boat caught up in a violent storm, the dandelions whirling in the wind, the vessel almost capsizing, water filling the boy's mouth. I name him "Cuba" because that is where I heard he went to after Baby She's parents talked her into marrying the baker's son. I imagine Baby She growing old, standing in the doorway, the way Madda Shilling stands watching the sky - her head fluffy and white, the evening breeze making little puffs at it.

At the bottom of the page, I write "The End," but the story does not want to end. I find myself drawing dandelions in the margins of the notebook; I embellish each sheet with flying chutes, sketch between each line.

2. Nights I dream of women filing into Madda's yard, come to lively up the eggs that doctor says are no good, their ovaries bursting open fluffy as dandelions.

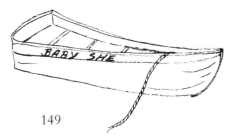

149

C. Natural Herstory I

1. One day while walking along the beach, Girl asks, Why does the sea taste like salt? I have to admit, I do not know the answer.

2. But here it is: Sea salt comes from stones. Stones are made of mineral salts and when over time they dissolve with acid rain, the salt is washed down from the bottoms of rivers, all the way out to the bright blue sea.

3. Salt never evaporates.

4. "Is that the truth, Mama?" Girl asks.

5. The truth is the sea is full of stories and sometimes stories taste like salt.

D. Natural Herstory II

As far as I can tell, Madda Shilling's butterfly was of the Giant Swallowtail species, *Papilio humerus.* With a wing span of six inches, this swallowtail is endemic to Jamaica and one of the largest butterflies in the world.

   At the moment of Madda's death, the swallowtail butterfly released itself from her neck and flew away, caught up by air current. Later, it hung for days, from a mahoe tree, its wings closed, before attaching itself to someone else – a young girl washing her face in a plastic basin in a yard filled with pepper plants and tomato vines. The girl stopped and peered over her shoulder, smiling. But then when the butterfly did not move, she ran inside the house calling, Mommy! The mother beat the girl's back with a kitchen towel, cussing the butterfly in Jesus name back to dutty hell, until reluctantly if flew away. Many are called, but few are chosen.

I recently spoke to the girl, now a grown woman, at her home in Mandeville. Suffice to say that after the experience out in the yard, she took to researching butterflies and dragonflies and doctor birds and all manner of flying things. Her work has appeared under various names in books and journals on Jamaican fauna.

In gathering material for this story, I wanted so much to see the Giant Swallowtail first hand. In December of 2001, I hiked with a cousin through the John Crow Mountains for a full day. We found much of interest that day – wild hog, rare orchids – but no Giant Swallowtails. We were disappointed, but not surprised, the species is, after all, endangered. I returned to the mountains with friends the following year. Just as we were about to return to the car, someone shouted, and for one full minute, I was mesmerized, black and gold wings brushing past my head before floating off into the distance, disappearing into the green. *Papilio humerus,* I rolled it over my tongue. So majestic it was and so confident in its flight. For two days, I was too moved to write anything at all. This for me was the whole meaning of story.

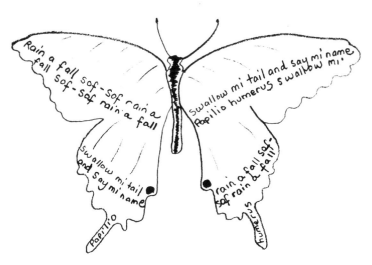

E. Natural Herstory III

1. There are over 500 species of snails in Jamaica, 90% of which are endemic. Jamaica also has the highest density of snails in the world. But given Madda Shilling's story, is it any wonder there are so many snails on this island?

2. A snail's shell contains calcium carbonate from sources such as soil or limestone. The snail woman must therefore feed herself a diet rich in this nutrient. I have known snail women to crush a little limestone and mix it in with the flour or cornmeal used to make fried dumplings. I have also known women to gather tiny bits of gravel from under trees or along the roadside.

3. At puberty, snail women automatically shift into survival mode. The shell begins to develop on the top of the head, right at the spot of the former fulcrum. As the shell grows, a series of rings appear, one ring for each year of growth.

4. Snail women are almost always of the left-handed or sinistral variety, that is, the whorls of the shell grow counterclockwise.

5. There is a short history of male snailing. During slavery, certain men in an attempt to cross ocean, developed conch. Conch were difficult to conceal and we know of only one man who made it all the way back to Ghana.

F. Things Found

June 3, 2002
Feathers in an old skirt pocket.

September 30, 2002
Bougainvillea in my address book.

November 26, 2002
Bird prints on the kitchen floor.

G. Things Lost

May 28, 2002
My favorite earrings.

H. Gifts Received

November 7, 2001
Milly's needle.

January 1, 2003
I have opened the present Sister left for me on the windowsill. It is her finger – the one Massa cut off – dried up now and stiff. I wear it in an amulet around my neck.

June 9, 2003
A dandelion from Girl.

I. Miscellaneous Darlings

1. "...her toenails like little moons waxing and waning on Madda's tile floor."

2. "Stop now and come to bed..." (Coopie)

3. One coconut tree leaning to the side. (View from the kitchen)

4. "See how I hang like pink frangipani." (Mrs. Ying)

5. Girl and her stuffed rabbit silhouetted against the window.

J. Translation of Mrs. Ying's Note (Written on the Morning of her Death)

One day, not now, I will return –
second chance tied around my waist,
little bells announcing my name.

有一天,雖然不是現在,但我將會回來
在我身上圍繞著另一種希望
小小的鈴鐺為我的名而歌唱

J (b). Recipe for the Coconut Drops in Mrs. Ying's Showcase

1 diced coconut
3/4 pound brown sugar

1 teaspoon grated ginger
vanilla to taste
a little salt
Boil all ingredients for half an hour. Use a spoon to drop
onto a greased surface. Let dry. Yields 12.

K. <u>Willa's Chant</u>

an ting an
ting
an
ting an ting
an ting
an
ting down slow
ting
down slow
ting

down slow
Jahtings

(Audio/ 28 seconds)

L. <u>View from the Edge of the World</u>

Not even God-self know what really going on this
little mango island. Hail Mary out in the yard,
dancing between wet sheets on the line, hallelujah;
the messiah's heart beating fast, beating fast.

CSIS

M. HER CURIOUS BOOK, as it were, or; Storyteller Contemplates the Eye of a Needle.

I am standing on the spot where Blue saw the birds swirling overhead. There is a funeral in progress on the far southeast corner and I hear relatives of the deceased, their songs rising up like on the Day of Pentecost.

It is evening and the breeze finds a home in my hair. My lips are moist, the stone dislodged from my throat, all my years turning like pages, my breath slowing and quickening to the rhythm of the text.

Sister Story-Ma

Alva

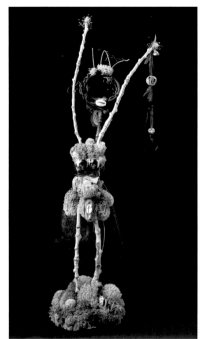

Dahlia

Made in China

Millie Donovan

Willa

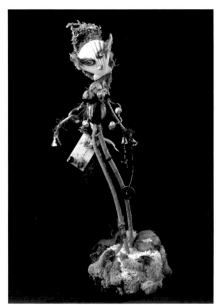

Mrs Ying

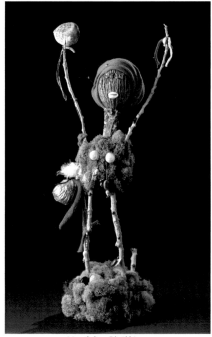

Madda Shilling

Marion Tate Rice a.k.a "Bad rice"
(Photograph from the *Gleaner* – August 18, 2002)

Marcia Douglas was born in the UK of Jamaican parents in 1961, but grew up in rural Jamaica. She left Jamaica in 1990 to study for a Master of Fine Arts in Creative Writing at Ohio State University and was awarded a Ph D in African American and Caribbean Literature in 1997.

Her first publications appeared in *Sister of Caliban: A Multilingual Anthology of Contemporary Caribbean Women Poets* (1996) and in *Callaloo*, *Sun Dog: Southeast Review*, *Phoebe* and *APTE*.

Her first collection of poems, *Electricity Comes to Cocoa Bottom* (Peepal Tree, 1999) won a Poetry Book Society recommendation. It explores the recuperation of Jamaican place and voice from the perspective of a young woman in urban America in resistance to culturally annihilating forces in that society.

In 2000, she published her first novel, *Madam Fate* with The Women's Press. Since then her fiction has been published in *Whispers from the Cotton Tree Root: Caribbean Fabulist Fiction*. Invisible Cities Press, 2000; *The Edexcel Anthology for GCSE English*. Ed. Anna Maloney. Hodder & Stoughton Educational, 2002; and *Mojo: Conjure Stories.* Ed. Nalo Hopkinson. Warner Books, 2003.

She currently lives in Boulder, Colorado with her daughter, Avani. She lectures at the University of Colorado.

Electricity Comes to Cocoa Bottom
ISBN 1900715287, £7.99

Electricity Comes to Cocoa Bottom takes the reader on a journey of light, from the flicker of the firefly in rural Jamaica, through the half-moonlight of the limbo of exile in the USA to the point of arrival and reconnection imaged by the eight-pointed star.

It is also a journey of the voice, traversing back and forth across the Atlantic and across continents, pushing its way through word censors and voice mufflers and ending in tongues of fire.

In making this book a Poetry Book Society recommendation, its selector commented: 'Marcia Douglas has the kind of intent but relaxed concentration which ushers the reader into the life of a poem and makes the event - a wedding, a hot afternoon, an aeroplane journey - seem for a while like the centre of things. This is a rich and very welcome book.'

June Owens writes in *The Caribbean Writer*: 'Some writers leave their creative handprints in dark caves where only later happenstance may, perhaps, discover them. Some writers stamp their entire selves upon the language, upon a culture, upon literature and upon our consciousness in so intimate, singular, well-illumined and indelible a manner that there can be no mistaking their poems and prose for those of another. Such a writer is Marcia Douglas.'